Nick Caistor has been working with Latin American literature for fifteen years. He edited the English version of ¡*Nunca Más*!, the report on the disappeared people in Argentina, as well as *The Faber Book of Contemporary Latin American Stories*. He has also translated work by the Argentine writer Osvaldo Soriano, the Nicaraguan novelist Sergio Ramírez and the Uruguayan Juan Carlos Onetti.

Columbus' Egg

New Latin American Stories on
the Conquest

Selected and edited by Nick Caistor

faber and faber
BOSTON · LONDON

"Chac Mool" is from *Burnt Water* and is reprinted by kind permission of Farrar, Straus & Giroux, and Secker and Warburg. English translation © 1980.
"Axolotl", from *End of the Game* (1968), is reprinted by kind permission of Collins Harvill.
Juan Goytisolo's afterword originally appeared in *El País*.

This edition published in the United States in 1992 by Faber and Faber, Inc., 50 Cross Street, Winchester, MA 01890.
First published in Great Britain in 1992 by Serpent's Tail, 4 Blackstock Mews, London N4 2BT.

Published by arrangement with Serpent's Tail Ltd.

A CIP record for this book is available from the Library of Congress.

ISBN 0-571-19799-X

Printed in the United Kingdom.

Contents

For Amanda:
"consummation and freedom".

I have always read that the world comprising the land and the water was spherical, as is testified by the investigations of Ptolemy and others, who have proved it by the eclipses of the moon, and other observations made from east to west, as well as by the elevation of the pole from north to south. But I have now seen so much irregularity, as I have already described, that I have come to another conclusion respecting the earth, namely, that it is not round as they describe, but of the form of a pear, which is very round except where the stalk grows, at which part it is most prominent; or like a round ball, upon one part of which is a prominence like a woman's nipple, this protrusion being the highest and nearest the sky, situated under the equinoctial line, and at the eastern extremity of this sea — I call that the eastern extremity, where the land and the islands end.

Christopher Columbus:
Letter to the Royal Highnesses, Third Voyage

Columbus being at a party with many noble Spaniards, where, as was customary, the subject of the conversation was the Indies, one of them undertook to say: "Señor Cristobal, even if you had not undertaken this great enterprise, we should not have lacked a man who would have made the same discovery that you did, here in our own country of Spain, as it is full of great men clever in cosmography and literature." Columbus made no reply, but took an egg and had it placed on the table, saying: "Gentlemen, you make it stand here, not with crumbs, salt, etc. (for anyone knows how to do it with meal and sand), but naked and without anything at all, as I will, who was the first to discover the Indies." They all tried, and no one succeeded in making it stand up. When the egg came round to the hands of Columbus, by beating it down on the table he fixed it, having thus crushed a little of one end; wherefore all remained confused, understanding what he meant: that after the deed is done, everybody knows how to do it; that they ought first to have sought for the Indies, and not laugh at him who had sought for them first.

Benzoni: *Historia del Mondo Nuovo,* 1565

Introduction

Three snapshots. In the first, I am visiting the ruined temple of Monte Albán in the state of Oaxaca, Mexico, with a coachload of Latin American tourists. One of them, an elderly Argentine gent, is indignant at the ruins. "Look what those Spaniards did," he protests, "destroying a civilization like that." "Yes," retorts an equally elderly Mexican standing next to him, raising himself to his full height and dignity, "and they created me." In the second, I am in Chile at a drunken evening of guitar music and poetry. A Chilean friend, with coppery skin, dark brown eyes and jet black hair, reads a passionate poem in honour of the oneness of all America. Afterwards, a woman comes up to him and tipsily remarks how handsome and "indian" he looked reciting his poem. "I'm no indian," the poet snaps. "My grandparents were from the Canary Islands and Spain." For the third, we are experiencing the carnival in Bolivia. We've left the tourists behind, and finally think we have made it to a place where the authentic, autochthonous celebrations are going on. We push our way through to join in the fun — to be pelted with a mixture of chicha beer and flour, driven out to the sound of cackling laughter, drenched and made to look even whiter and more foolish.

This mixture of Latin American reactions to themselves, their own past, and to others is particularly relevant in this year of the 500th anniversary of Columbus' discovery of their continent. Latin Americans have as many problems coming to terms with their legacy from pre-Columbian times as they do with their place in the world since the arrival of the Spaniards. They came into being as a mistake and as the result of violence. Columbus thought he was discovering a quick way to the East, with the consequence that, from the beginning, Latin American identity has been plagued with this fear that "perhaps it was all a terrible mistake". Columbus compounded this mistake as the continent's first fictional writer. The journals of his voyages and the letters he wrote to the Spanish monarchs are such a mixture of fact, dogmatic argument and fantasy that they can almost be said to be the distant forerunner of a whole school of 20th-century writing on the continent. Perhaps imagination, as ever, can rescue even the worst mistakes.

As well as being a mistake, the birth of Latin America was a violent, illegitimate one. Malinche, the interpreter and mistress to Hernán Cortés, the Spanish conqueror of Mexico, is the best image of this. She gave symbolic birth to the new peoples of the continent, doomed to feel they belonged neither to the old world of America before it was so named, nor the old world of Europe they had also left behind. The original inhabitants of the continent are the legitimate ones; the newcomers have only their violence and spleen, like that of Edmund in *King Lear*, roaring: "Why brand they us/ with base? with baseness? bastardy? base, base?/ Who in the lusty stealth of nature take/ more composition and fierce quality/ Than doth, within a dull, stale, tired bed,/Go to th'creating a whole tribe of fops,/Got 'tween asleep and wake?" This sense has provoked many violent attempts to assert their own identity, whatever the cost to others or to themselves.

The 500th anniversary of Columbus' stumbling on the edge of the Latin American continent has stirred up this debate on Latin American identity yet again. It seemed a useful contribution to look at how contemporary writers of fiction in Spanish from the region see the question and the emotions it rouses. I have no competence to understand or translate the descendants of the peoples who originally lived on the continent, nor do I feel it is possible or honest to speak on their behalf. Most of the stories in this collection are appearing for the first time in English; some were suggested by the authors themselves, some were written especially for this book. I begin and end the selection with stories by two writers who are dead now, but whose work in many ways straddles the debate. On the one hand, Miguel Angel Asturias, the great Guatemalan writer who won the Nobel Prize for Literature long before Gabriel

García Márquez. His work is often an attempt to recreate the spirit and ethos of the world that was lost with the arrival of the Spaniards, to make it valid and valuable not as folklore but as something alive for now. On the other, the Argentine writer Julio Cortázar, who keenly felt throughout his life the double pull of America and Europe and who, in his short story 'Axolotl', gives his version of the Mexican hybrid that my coach tour companion felt himself to be.

Nick Caistor

*Legend of the Treasure
in the Place of Flowers*

Miguel Angel Asturias

*S*lowly, drop by drop, daylight was draining from the damp city walls, like a fire consumed in its embers. An orange-peel sky, with streaks of pitahaya blood among the clouds, here red, there the yellow of maize husk or the hide of a puma.

High on the temple roof, a lookout saw a cloud glide over the lake, almost kissing the water, then stretch out at the foot of the volcano. As soon as the priest saw its eyes close, he ran down into the temple, his cloak billowing behind him, shouting that war was over. At the end of each shout, his arms dropped to his sides like the wings of a bird; each time he drew breath he raised them again. In the temple yard on the west, the sun's beard, the stones of the city, were flecked with something dying . . .

Messengers sped forth to announce to the four winds that war was over in all the lands of the lords of Atitlan.

That night a great fair was held. The lake was covered with lights. The traders' boats plied across the water, lit like stars. Boats of fruit sellers. Boats of sellers of clothes and footwear. Boats of sellers of jade, emeralds, pearls, gold dust, feather quills filled with perfumed waters, reed armbands. Boats of sellers of honey, chillis and chilli powders, salt and precious copal resins. Boats of sellers of dyes and plumage. Boats of sellers of turpentine, medicinal leaves and roots. Boats of sellers of fowl. Boats of sellers of maguey ropes, rush matting, slings, pine shavings, large and small pots, hides cured and raw, urns and stone masks. Boats of sellers of macaws, parrots, coconuts, fresh resin, gourds with soft seeds . . .

The daughters of the great lords went by, watched over by the priests, in canoes lit like ears of white corn. The sounds of the musicians and singers accompanying the city's leading families alternated with the traders' sharp, skilful bargaining.

None of this tumult ruffled the night. It was like a floating market of people asleep, buying and selling in their dreams. The cocoa seeds they used for money changed hands without a sound across the clusters of boats and men.

The birdsellers' boats brought the song of the mocking-birds, the stentorian cries of orioles, the chatter of parakeets . . . They cost whatever the buyer was willing to pay, but never less than twenty seeds, because the birds were love offerings.

All round the lakeshore, the lights and whispers of the loving couples and the birdsellers rippled and died away among the trees.

Daybreak found the priests high in the pine branches observing the volcano. The oracle of peace and war: shrouded in cloud, it offered peace and security to this Place of Flowers; standing out clearly it presaged war, foreign invasion. Overnight, while sunflowers and humming birds slept, the volcano had been fleeced with clouds.

So it was peace. There would be more celebrations. The priests were preparing for sacrifices in the temple, making ready garments, altars, obsidian knives. Flutes, shells, all kinds of drum were played. The thrones of honour had been set up. There were flowers, fruit, birds, honeycombs, feathers, gold, precious stones to offer the warriors as reward. Canoes shot back and forth from the lakeshore, ferrying people whose rainbow-coloured clothes gave them the appearance of flowers. In the silences, the voices of the priests rang out, priests with yellow mitres who lined the staircases of Atit's temple like gold braid.

"Our hearts rested in the shade of our lances!" the priests proclaimed. "The insides of our trees, of our houses, were filled with the remains of animals, eagle and jaguar!"

"There goes the leader! That's him! The one over there!" seemed to be the cry from the city elders, bearded like gods of old: "There goes the leader! That's him! The one over there!"

"I can see my son, over there, look, in that column!" the mothers cried, their eyes as gentle as water from so many tears.

"That one," the young girls interrupted them, "he is the one all our eyes are on, with his puma mask and the red feathers of his heart!"

And to another group, as they passed by, "He is the lord of our days! His golden mask, his feathers of the sun!"

The mothers recognized their sons among the warriors by the masks they wore; the young girls were told by their maids which costumes their heroes were wearing.

They pointed out the leader: "That's him! Can't you see his chest, as red as blood, his arms green like the blood of plants? The blood of trees, blood of animals! He is bird and tree! Can't you see the light shimmering on his dove's body? Can't you see the plumes of his tail? Bird with green blood! Tree with red blood! Kukul! It's him, it's him!"

The warriors marched past in squads of twenty, fifty, a hundred, according to their plumes' hue. After a squadron of twenty warriors in red costumes and plumes came fifty dressed in green, then a hundred in yellow feathers. Then the soldiers decked out in multicoloured feathers like the macaw, the bird of deceit. A rainbow with a hundred feet . . .

"Four women clad in cotton jerkins and carrying arrows! They fought as valiantly as four young men!" The voices of the priests rang out above the crowd, who were shouting as if they were mad outside the temple to Atit, overflowing with flowers, bunches of fruit: women with breasts painted and tipped like spears.

In the decorated bowl of the baths, the leader received the messengers, the men of Castile sent by Pedro de Alvarado. He greeted them with warm words, and had them killed on the spot. Then, with red plumes on his chest and green ones on both arms, wearing a cloak embroidered with iridescent wing feathers, his head uncovered and on his feet only a pair of golden sandals, he joined the celebrations with the elders, the councillors, the priests. Red clay on one shoulder feigned a wound; on his fingers he wore so many rings that his hands seemed like sunflowers.

The warriors danced in the square in front of the temple, shooting arrows at the garlanded prisoners of war tied to tree trunks. As the leader passed by, a priest of sacrifice dressed in black placed a blue arrow in his hands.

The sun shot its arrows at the city, firing them from the bow of the lake . . .

The birds shot their arrows at the lake, firing them from the bow of the woods . . .

The warriors shot their arrows at the prisoners, careful not to kill them, so that the celebrations and their agony would go on. . .

The chief drew back his bow with the blue arrow, aiming at the youngest prisoner, to mock him, to adore him. Immediately the other warriors pierced him with their arrows, from near and far, dancing to the beat of the drums.

All at once, a lookout ran in. Panic took hold of the crowd. The speed and force with which the volcano was tearing the clouds apart meant a powerful army on the march against the city. The volcano crater stood out ever more clearly. Twilight had left something on the cliffs of the distant coast that was dying without a murmur, like the white shapes that until a minute before had been motionless, but now were caught up in the general ruin. Torches snuffed out in the streets . . . the doves lamenting under the tall pines . . . free of cloud, the volcano spoke of war!

"I fed you too poorly from my house, the honey I collected for you was not enough; for you I would have won the city, together we would have been rich!" the priests cried from their fortress, their anointed hands stretched out to the volcano, shining through the magic mists of the lake. The warriors made ready and said:

"May the white men fall into confusion at the sight of our weapons! May our shimmering feathers never fail us, the arrow, flower and torment of Spring! May our lances wound without wounding!"

The white men were advancing, barely visible in the mist. Were they phantoms or living beings? The earth swallowed up all sound of their drums, their trumpets, their marching feet. They came on with no trumpets, no footsteps, no drums.

Battle was joined in the maizefields. The men of the Place of Flowers fought long and hard. In defeat they fell back on the city, ringed by walls of cloud like Saturn.

The white men came on with no sound of trumpets, footsteps or drums. Their swords, breastplates, their lances, their horses barely visible through the mist. They swept down on the city like a storm, tossing out clouds, paying no heed to danger, sweeping all before them, iron men, unassailable, surrounded by flashes of light from the gleaming fire that sprang from their hands like fleeting fireflies. Some of the tribe undertook the defence; others fled across the lake with the treasure of the Place of Flowers to the foot of the volcano on the far shore, fled in boats that the invaders, lost in their adamantine sea of clouds, mistook for explosions of precious stones in the distance.

There was no time to burn the tracks. The trumpets sounded! The drums were beating! The walls of the city were shredded like clouds on the white men's spears; then they too rushed on from the abandoned city, rushed to use tree trunks as boats in their pursuit of the tribe burying the treasure. The trumpets sounded! The drums were beating! The sun shone fiercely on the farmers' fields. The islands of the lake shook with emotion, like the hands of the priests stretched out towards the volcano.

The trumpets sounded! The drums were beating!

At the first shots from the arquebuses, the tribe fled down mountain gorges, leaving behind pearls, diamonds, emeralds, opals, rubies, amethysts, gold discs, gold dust, gold figures, idols, jewels, silver mounts and supports, gold goblets and plate, blowpipes covered with pearls and precious stones, rock crystal basins, fine garments and instruments, yard upon yard of fabric embroidered with rich feathers; mounds of treasure that the invaders gazed on in amazement from their boats, already disputing their share of the booty. They headed for shore. The trumpets sounded! The drums were beating! Suddenly they heard the volcano drawing breath. The slow breathing of the Grandfather of the Waters halted them for a while, but soon, ready for anything, they followed the wind to try a second time to disembark and seize the treasure. A torrent of fire barred their way. Like the spit of a giant toad. The trumpets fell silent! The drums were stilled! Ashes floated on the waters like rubies, the sun's rays were hard as diamonds; scorched in their suits of armour, their ships drifting helpless, Pedro de Alvarado's men stared petrified with fear, livid with rage, at this insult the elements were heaping on them, as the volcano threw mountain on mountain, jungle on jungle, river upon cascading river, showers of rocks, flames, ashes, lava, sand, floods, heaping another volcano on top of the treasure of the Place of Flowers, laid by the tribe at its feet, like a twilight.

Translated by Nick Caistor

Paramnesia

Juan José Saer

One sees nothing in the sun but what is real.
Quevedo, *Marco Bruto*

For Jorge Conti

*I*n the slow, windless dawn, the smoke from the fire he had just lit rose and dispersed, intricate and indolent, more languid even than at dusk the day before, and the captain noticed the smell of the smoke and the fire but not the stench of death that came in gusts from the square courtyard of the fort, just as he heard the murmur of the sputtering firewood but not the cries, moans and curses of the two dying men. But the previous evening was now just a dead glow, precise and fantastic; its lifeless image wandered in and out of the darkness in the captain's mind whilst he clung to the physical proximity of the fire, so erratic and changeable now that even when its mad flames flickered over his face and motionless body as he crouched nearby, transfixed, something in the air told him that before the sun had risen very much higher the flames would have died down completely and the fire gone out. The heat of the day had been so intense that the captain was no longer even aware of it; if he had been, he would have made the most of the feeble and somewhat irritating cool of dawn, rather than sitting down beside the fire. Though he had hardly slept and so had no sense of any transition from one day to the next, he could clearly perceive the gradual moment by moment transformations and see how those minute modifications were causing everything to change and disappear. The tiniest detail, something no one else would have noticed, was enough. And when he crossed that strange desert strewn with corpses, when he walked up from the yellow beach to the group of half-ruined buildings made of adobe and rough timber that they called the fort or stronghold (though to the casual observer the overwhelming impression was one of fragility) the captain sensed that, however hard he tried, there was nothing he could do to prevent those changes: someone would die suddenly (there were only two others left, apart from himself), gangrene would spread and an arm that only yesterday evening had been flesh pink would turn black; rains would fall, changing the colour of sand and trees, the sun would rise, blazing down ever more intensely as midday approached, and then begin to wane until at last nightfall brought extinction. The captain was squatting down, utterly still, watching the fire; his huge, dark eyes shone, reflecting the flames, the one clearly discernible feature in a head otherwise obscured by a tangle of black hair and beard and the crust of dried mud that had been caked on his skin for some days now.

Dead leaves covered the ground beneath the semicircle of trees that edged the broad clearing near the riverbank, the clearing in which the fort had been built. However, these were not the golden leaves of April and May that fall naturally and spontaneously, but a dusty carpet of grey and withered leaves seared by the fierce mid-February heat. When he walked over to the trees to stand in the shade and watch the sun beating down on the huddle of crudely constructed, round-roofed buildings encircled by a stockade made from sticks, he would hear the scrunch and crackle of leaves crumpling beneath the weight of his boots. The trees would seem darker in the dawn and, against the brightening sky, each leaf would be surrounded by a nimbus of light. But that was not what the captain was seeing now; he was outside the stockade, near the entrance, squatting down with his back to the fort and his face towards the river from which he was separated by the big fire and a wide expanse of sandy beach. The captain thought he could remember the sound the leaves made when he trod on them with his boots, or rather with what remained of his boots. "It's possible to get up and walk over there," he thought, "walk over the leaves and hear them crackle beneath your feet." He could not get the idea out of his head. "What's more," he thought, "it's possible to get up, walk over there and, standing in the shade and looking back, see the whole fort. I'll go over there when the sun comes up, I'll look back and see the fort and the stretch of beach separating it from the river." He stayed there for nearly an hour, unmoving, immersed in thought. To anyone watching he would have seemed not even to be breathing, although from time to time, at irregular intervals, his great, dark eyes would widen a little, he would give a troubled frown and emit long, deep sighs like wordless responses to the speckles of pale phosphorescent light that flickered inside his mind; he sat watching the fire, his elbows resting on his thighs and his face cupped in his hands, and when he finally got up, although he had not actually slept, he had a sense again of having let his guard drop, for the sun was now high in the sky and all that remained of the spluttering flames was a layer of ash just thick enough to conceal the fire's one tiny dying ember. Once he was on his feet he noticed the long shadow he cast and noticed too that he had been sitting in the shade of the stockade, a shade broken regularly by the straight strips of sunlight that slipped between the posts. He thought: "When I turn round, my shadow will follow me." Then he heard a sudden moan from one of the dying men and recognized in that muted sound the peculiar timbre of the priest's voice. The captain went into the fort, then stopped, and his shadow stopped behind him. The priest was slumped in the middle of the square courtyard; he was surrounded by corpses and was the object of contemplation of the red-bearded soldier who was still sitting on the ground, his hands resting limply on his knees, his back against the base of one of the adobe huts. The captain shook his head and walked over to the priest who was grimacing in pain as he attempted to pull himself up into a sitting position; he kept opening and closing his eyes as if he found even breathing an effort. The captain crouched down beside him, staring at him and smiling.

"For the love of God, bring me some water," said the priest.

"No," said the captain.

"Please, for the love of God," said the priest in a weak voice.

"Die," said the captain, "die, you villain."

He stood up again and went over to the redheaded soldier who was watching him from a distance.

"And you!" the captain shouted.

The soldier seemed not to hear. The captain went over to him. His boots thudded and rang on earth beaten hard by months of coming and going by the feet of those now dead. The captain listened carefully to the sound of his own steps and even slowed his pace to hear them better; for a moment he almost relaxed and forgot the question he had just formulated inside himself and which he intended putting to the soldier. When he reached the soldier's side, he bent over him and paused. Then he smiled again, a smile full of false joviality.

"Where are you from?" he asked.

"I've told you a hundred times already, captain," said the soldier, "I'm from Segovia."

"You're lying."

"You've got the devil in you," said the soldier, "Either that or you are the Devil."

"Tell me about Segovia," said the captain.

"So you are the Devil," said the soldier.

"Tell me about Madrid," said the captain.

The soldier said nothing and continued looking across at the priest. His red beard and hair were dull and dirty, his skin densely freckled and there were bluish circles around his eyes. Above his own tangled, mud-spattered beard the captain's eyes glinted. "I'll get up now, I'll go out of the fort and I'll walk over to the trees," he thought; then, almost to himself, he murmured: "Die."

He stood up. The sun shone full in his face. Though shrunken and shrivelled by hunger, the captain's stocky, compact body was still strong. Whenever he stood up he held his arms slightly bent at his sides as if at any moment he were about to rest his hands on his hips; the sun in his eyes made him keep up a rapid blinking that lent him a general air of perplexity. He recalled the image of the fort as seen from the trees, as the indians would have seen it ten days ago when they watched from the woods awaiting their moment to attack and sacrifice them all like animals: the stockade made of pointed sticks, above which could be seen the round straw roofs and, above them, the tops of the trees on the far side of the woods forming a semicircle around the site, and to the right, the sandy beach sloping gently down to the river. The captain shook his head as if waking from some kind of dream. He addressed the soldier again.

"Do you know the king?" he said.

"The Devil will come and carry you off, captain," said the soldier. He spoke in a faint voice, without even looking at him. In fact, he wasn't really looking at anything and he only appeared to be looking at the priest because of the stiff, unnatural angle at which his head was resting against the wall of the hut and which left his eyes trained in that direction; indeed such was the stolid indifference with which he watched the priest's slow-motion attempts to sit up, the two of them might been living on different planets. The priest was so thin he looked like a dark stain left on the earth by some viscous substance obstinately resisting absorption and capable of a few freakish movements.

"And the indians will make stew out of you," said the captain, laughing. "Do you want some water?"

"No, captain," said the soldier. "Give it to the priest, he was the one who asked you for it. If you give the priest some water, I'll tell you about the king."

The captain scanned his face.

"Tell me first," he said.

"No," said the soldier.

Now the captain had stopped looking at the red-bearded soldier lying on the ground. He was on his feet again, his head up, and thus unable to see him, not that he showed the slightest interest in doing so. His gaze seemed to bounce off the scorched wall of a half burned-out hut, its straw roof caved in and full of holes, blackened by smoke and fire. The captain gave the impression that he knew in advance what the soldier's answers would be and that he was only asking the questions for the pleasure of hearing the same replies repeated again and again.

"No," he said, "tell me first."

The redheaded soldier said nothing. He was about fifty years old, but the freckles and the sickly pallor that refracted the sun's fiery rays gave him a look of vacuous innocence; one glance, though, showed that he was in fact old enough to be the captain's father. The captain was waiting. The sun fell full on his face now and the fragile cool of dawn had vanished or been tempered by the growing heat of the morning, as the sun rose in a sky of faded blue, without a single cloud, not even a haze of cirrus, on the horizon; but the air was not dry, it was humid and sticky. In another hour the sweat would begin making dark trails in the crust of dried mud clinging to the captain's face. The captain's expression did not change or, if it did, the change was so infinitesimal as to pass unnoticed beneath the dirty, curly beard. The red-bearded soldier still said nothing. At last, the captain looked about him and, spotting a battered jug on the ground near the priest, he went over and picked it up. He walked past the priest without even looking at him and left the fort; his long, stiff shadow went before him, stretching out across the sandy soil. The captain's tattered boots sank into the sand, forcing him to take long, energetic strides. "Now I'm going towards the river," he thought. But he did not think this with anything resembling words, rather he was suddenly filled by the pure sensation of going, by a sense at that particular moment of simply putting one foot forward and then the other, of alternately plunging first one foot, then the other into the sand, each foot encased in its tattered boot. He stopped and turned round, looking back at the deep tracks he had left in the sand; the whole area was full of those tracks, coming from all directions and intersecting to form an intricate diagram. They looked like small craters opening up on a lunar surface. The captain kept on walking until he reached the river; one might have said the water was utterly still, with no hint of a current in either direction, or even that it wasn't water at all, were it not for the almost imperceptible lapping of the water on the shore, revealing a narrow fringe of firm, damp sand each time it withdrew; it could have been mistaken for a smooth stretch of brown earth but for the intense glitter of sunlight on its surface. The captain bent over the opaque waters and filled the jug without even bothering to rinse it out first. He did not pause to fill it, but stooped down, plunging the battered jug into the water and drawing it out full as he turned to go back towards the fort. When the captain swung the jug up again, the water that spilled out sparkled for a fraction of a second then fell back into the river with a loud, crystalline splash. "Now I'm going back to the fort," thought the captain, and set off, followed by his shadow. When he trod too heavily, his foot became stuck fast in the sand, making him totter and stumble so that water slopped out of the brimming jug; the drops fell to earth only to be instantly absorbed, leaving large, round stains on the sand. The captain went back into the fort and crouched down by the priest.

"Here, drink," he said, handing him the jug. "Drink it and die."

"You'll have to help him, captain," shouted the soldier, "the father can't manage on his own."

The captain put an arm round the priest's shoulders and held the jug to his lips. The water ran down from the corners of his mouth into his beard and stained his ragged habit. The captain, though unsolicitous, was not ungentle, but when he saw that the priest was now vomiting the few drops of water he had managed to drink, he threw down the jug and left the priest lying on the ground in the sun. The captain went over to the redheaded soldier and squatted down in front of him, looking straight at him.

"Talk," he said.

The other man did not even look at him.

"It was just before the levy that brought me here," he said. "I was in the country one day, near the high road, and I saw a great procession of coaches and horses approaching, carrying all kinds of flags. Thinking it must be some nobleman, I stopped to look. The first coach was guarded by soldiers bearing pikes and banners." The soldier fell silent and looked at the captain.

"Aren't you going to bury the dead, captain? It stinks around here."

The captain's eyes glinted.

"Go on," he said.

The soldier looked away again.

"The first coach went past and then the one behind it lost a wheel and overturned in front of me. Several gentlemen were thrown out and the coachman landed right at my feet. He lay there crossing himself and weeping. The coaches following behind passed by and then stopped and people started to get out: captains, dukes, courtiers, people like that, captain. The ones who'd been thrown out started getting to their feet, helped by the others. And they're all talking excitedly, brushing down their clothes and adjusting their breeches, when the first coach comes back and stops in front of the others. A man gets out and behind him a bishop; everyone kneels down on the ground and so do I, just in case. The nobleman asks if anyone is badly hurt and when everyone says no, he goes over to the coachman, who's trembling from head to foot by now, and he says: 'You overturned that coach with such style, sir, anyone would think you'd done it before.' Everyone laughed. So did I. Then the king told everyone to continue on their way, that the sea awaited them, and disappeared back into his coach together with the bishop. And the coachman explained to me that they were noblemen carrying ammunition to the southern coast of Spain to help in the fight against the Moors. Then along came the levy that brought me here. Listen, captain, couldn't you at least throw a bit of sand over the dead?"

The captain was looking at him hard, but the soldier seemed not to notice: he had told his story with an ineffable calm and indifference and something akin to hopelessness. The captain gave him a look of mingled incredulity and scorn and stood up. He moved off thoughtfully, taking long strides, shaking his head. He left the fort and, without a backward glance, went off towards the wood. Even the tattered cambric shirt, half-unbuttoned to reveal the dense, dark hair on his chest, even that seemed to weigh on him. Sweat gleamed on his forehead. His boots sank into the sand, leaving deep tracks. The captain stopped and turned to look back at the river. It was so still and smooth that its presence was betrayed only by the shimmering light and what looked like pale golden dust sown in eddies on its surface by the sun. The opposite shore formed a bank, not a gently sloping beach, and because the river appeared and disappeared round steep curves in either direction, it did not look like a real river: its surface was more like that of waters confined within a narrow dock. It seemed to appear out of nowhere and to go nowhere, to consist of only that one visible fragment. And turning round and setting off again in the direction of the wood, the captain thought that was indeed how it seemed and that very probably it really did have neither origin nor continuation, that only what was there was real, and nothing else. The captain shook his head and gave a short laugh. "He told me about the king, about Segovia and Madrid," he thought. He went into the small wood and, in his tattered boots with their long, ragged laces, began walking over the dead leaves that covered the ground beneath the trees. Light seeped through the foliage, its rays fragmenting and falling obliquely onto trunks and branches. The withered leaves cracked and split. The wood fanned out from that first line of trees around the sandy clearing; it was full of trees so choked by climbing plants and creepers that they formed heavy, misshapen clumps of vegetation. The captain stopped and looked into the depths of the wood: not a leaf stirred in those dark, dense grottoes. He thought: "Now I'm going to turn round and I'm going to look back at the fort." He turned round and looked: there it was. Visible above the surrounding stockade of sharpened sticks, around which the wood formed a solid semicircle, were the main hut and the scorched and ravaged roofs of the derelict outbuildings; closer to the centre of that semicircle than to the river, the broad sweep of sand, yellow and blotched with white, sloped very gently, almost imperceptibly, away from the fort until it was lost in the water. The captain stood motionless, gazing unblinkingly at the scene laid out before him. Then two black birds flew by high overhead, flat against the blue sky, tracing a very slow, straight line. The captain followed them with his eyes until they disappeared from view. "They must be going somewhere," he thought. "There must be another place somewhere that they've come from. They must have come from somewhere else." But he did not think this with words; again he thought it with those specks of phosphorescent light that flickered inside his mind and which, though slow and ponderous in taking shape, were very quick to vanish. Once the birds had gone, the captain looked up at the sun. Its brilliance blinded him and, as he raised his head, a wave of still fierce heat seemed to run through him like an electrical charge, forcing him to screw his eyes tight shut and abruptly lower his head, leaving his retina dancing with scintillating points of light. He stood there for a moment, then opened his eyes again and walked on, stepping over the dried leaves that crunched and crumpled beneath his weight. The captain's breeches clung to his thighs and his tense muscles rippled as he moved. The captain walked round the edge of the wood until he was behind the rough construction they called the fort. There was only a short distance between the fort and the trees at that point. The captain could smell the stench of carrion. Although there was no wind, it came to him in gusts as if there were a sort of vent within his sense of smell that kept opening and closing at intervals, until the stench permeated everything and remained locked inside. Then he forgot about it and continued on. He walked around the whole semicircular edge of the wood and then returned to the fort. The priest was lying in the sun in exactly the same position as when the captain had left him; his breathing was so shallow his chest barely stirred. The redheaded soldier was still sitting with his back against the base of the hut. The captain squatted down next to the priest and, half closing his eyes, began to watch him; the priest's eyes were almost white, as if the pupils had been erased from them; close to, the captain noticed a change in the rhythm of the priest's breathing but could not judge if he was now taking longer to breathe out or to breathe in. The captain clenched his teeth.

Behind him the soldier cried out feebly: "For God's sake, captain, leave him in peace."

"How would you like me to cut off your head?" said the captain.

"I'd kiss your hands if you would, captain," said the soldier.

The soldier spoke without looking at him; he seemed to be contemplating something just above the captain's head, behind him, in the air, in the sky; the soldier was staring so hard at this that the tentative smile on the captain's face was instantly swallowed up into his beard and he turned his head sharply to look up in that direction; but he saw nothing, only the empty sky above the devastated buildings.

"How about *you* telling me the story about the king?" he said.

A murmur came from the priest's lips but the captain could not make out what it was.

"You'll have to speak up if you want me to hear you," said the captain.

The priest opened his mouth but no sound came out; he stayed like this, his mouth open, as if his jaw muscles had suddenly given out, and the eyes from which the pupils seemed to have been erased were white, as if coated with lacquer. The captain bent still closer, studying him. "Come on, tell me; you're supposed to be from Madrid, aren't you? Come on, spit it out," muttered the captain, in a voice taut with resentment. "Tell me the one about how there's an ocean and how we crossed it with the captain-general and how he sent us off on an expedition up here."

The captain spoke in a voice that was low and tense but at the same time clear and steady. The priest still did not move; he seemed to have lost the fragile appearance he had worn an hour before. His face was harder and darker and his breathing barely noticeable.

"Leave him in peace, captain," said the redheaded soldier in a faint voice, but the captain did not hear him. "You've got the devil in you, captain."

"Come on, tell me. Tell me," said the captain. "Tell me about the indians and their poison spears. Make me believe that all this is real. Make me believe that you and me and Judas over there haven't always been in this place, surrounded by rotting corpses; make me believe that there is somewhere other than this." He bent closer still, swaying to and fro on his haunches. "Make me believe it, you son of a whore," he said.

He stood up abruptly, assuming an air of both smugness and scorn. There was a kind of arrogance about him. His face burned in the sun and his forehead was beaded with sweat. Adopting a friendly expression, he went over to the redheaded soldier and sat down next to him. The soldier didn't move; his legs, stretched out in front of him, were so thin his boots looked as if they had nothing in them, as if there were no feet inside his battered footwear.

"Judas," said the captain affectionately, "I'm going to cut off your ears."

"It'll be yours they cut off, captain," said the soldier.

The captain burst out laughing. "You may be an old madman and a Judas born and bred," he said, "but I like you." He raised his head, tried to look directly into the sun again, but couldn't. "See, the sun still goes round. It still passes overhead just to make absolutely clear to us that we're here and nowhere else," he said. "And you talk to me about a king and a city that don't even exist. I ought to cut your tongue out for that."

"The priest has died," said the soldier, "I'm sure of it."

"Leave him in peace," said the captain.

"Aren't you going to give him a Christian burial?" said the soldier.

"Be quiet," said the captain.

They were not looking at each other. The soldier's gaze was still fixed on the same point in the empty sky above the huts and the captain was looking intently round the courtyard; the earth had been trodden hard by human feet and on it had been built the huts, with their straw roofs and adobe walls now in ruins, blighted by fire; the huts had not been laid out according to any particular plan and all were different, bearing only the slightest resemblance to one another; three of the five had been completely destroyed, their roofs collapsed and full of holes and the walls scorched and ravaged, and of the remaining two only one appeared to have survived intact, for the other was begrimed with black smoke that had issued forth from the hole in the wall that served as a doorway. Corpses disfigured by putrefaction lay about in various poses; two had spears buried in their chests. Far from the huts and the other bodies the priest lay motionless. He appeared to be dead. Beyond him was the entrance to the fort, the broad swathe of sand covered with footprints and, beyond that, the river. The captain suddenly swung round and leaned his back against the base of the hut, next to the redheaded soldier, so that he was shoulder to shoulder with him but looking in the opposite direction. They looked as if they were expecting something to descend from the sky; they were sweating.

"Would you like some quince jelly?" said the captain.

"No," said the soldier.

"What about some wine?" said the captain.

The soldier did not reply.

"Do you think he's dead? What's up, has the cat got your tongue?" said the captain. "Go on, go and tell the Holy Inquisition that I shit on God and all he stands for. Get on a ship, cross the ocean and go to your precious Madrid and tell them. Go on, go on; your Madrid is much more real than anything here."

The captain turned towards the soldier, who was sitting with his eyes open very wide.

"Is the sun bothering you?" he said. "It'll be gone soon."

His own eyes were beginning to burn and he rubbed them with his knuckles. When he lowered his fists, his eyes were red and watery. He opened and closed them, then blinked rapidly several times as if trying to demonstrate how fragile was the existence of all he saw. But everything was still unremittingly there; the captain raised his hand and with his fingertips felt the wall he was leaning against. That contact, he thought, when he lowered his hand, was now no more than a memory and if he were to reach out his hand again, the contact between wall and fingertips would be similar but different; of the first contact there would remain only a memory, that is to say, nothing. But that was an act of memory, not of recollection. He had only one recollection, which kept coming back to him, the recollection of something unknown, a recollection too feeble to carry with it the thing recollected and which lay instead jumbled and scattered amongst the trees and shrivelled leaves of the wood. The captain closed his eyes and the rhythm of his breathing changed, grew quieter. He was conscious of the sunlight beating on his face and the mute vigour with which his mud-caked beard and the pores of his skin seemed to bristle and creak; he was acutely aware of both this and the light whose glare penetrated even his tightly shut eyelids, wandering about behind them, until eventually darkness filled him and he fell asleep. He woke again almost at once and jumped to his feet, his hand on his empty sword belt. The redheaded soldier was looking directly at him — the first time he had done so — a bemused expression on his face. The captain's voice was hoarse.

"Did you hear something?" he said.

"The Devil in hell laughed at you and you heard him, captain," said the soldier.

"Shut your mouth," said the captain.

"You heard the Devil laughing and it woke you up," said the soldier.

He was no longer looking at the captain. His eyes were once more fixed on the same point they had been staring at all morning, and now his red beard gleamed from time to time as if repeatedly burnished by the sun. The captain took several paces in different directions and appeared not only to be re-identifying the place and his surroundings but also to be sniffing the air and looking up at both sun and sky, confirming with a glance that everything was as it should be and in its right place. He approached the priest and bent over him; although apparently dead, the priest was, in fact, still alive: he was barely breathing and though no light glimmered in his eyes, something in them had not yet died. Everything else in him was dead except for the shallow breathing and that something in his eyes. The captain stood up and spoke to the soldier.

"He's waiting for you. He told me they won't let him into hell unless you go with him," he said jovially, jerking his head in the direction of the priest.

His shirt was soaked in sweat and he ripped it off, tearing it into shreds as he did so. The skin on his chest and arms was burned black by the sun. He dried the sweat from his face and neck with a strip from the torn shirt, then threw it down. It fell onto the priest's leg; the captain did not even look at him; he walked out of the fort again, shaking his head and laughing. When he was outside he crouched down and picked up a handful of sand (the sand was hot; he had not expected that, but the contact would become memory the moment he let it go) then tossed it into the air. For a moment the light crackled and grew hazy in contrast with the millions of flying, falling particles that interrupted its monotonous intensity. The captain brushed his hand against his ragged breeches, then headed for the river and walked without a moment's hesitation into the water. As he advanced into the river he felt the drenching water gradually encroach — first upon his feet, then his calves, his knees, his thighs. Before the water had reached his waist he stopped and raised his arms, feeling the cold water cleaving to his body and noticing how the least movement renewed and revivified the icy shock. Then he dived in, rising into the air and arching his body in brief flight before plunging clamorously into the water, churning up the surface as he submerged himself. He swam for a time underwater, sightless and incapable of thought, holding his breath and moving through the turbid liquid, blinded and disoriented by the clouds of tumultuous red mud and the turbulent currents that produced a continual, dull murmur. He burst to the surface shaking his head and found himself facing the sandy beach and the fort and not, as he had expected, the islands near the farther shore. His hair clung to his skull and his beard, gushing water, converged, shining and smooth, to form a sharp point beneath his chin. Then he swam randomly about, first one way, then another, racing off in one direction only to turn sharply after two or three strokes, or changing position and style, filling the air with noise and splashing water that gleamed, transparent, in the sunlight. When he emerged from the water with slow, dragging steps, he dropped on to the sand and closed his eyes, letting the sun dry him. He lay stretched out on his back, his eyes closed. In his ears was a lingering echo of the noise his body had made as it hit the water and as he splashed and moved about in it. To rest more comfortably he placed his right forearm beneath his head. He was conscious of the contrast between the hot sand and his body cooled by the water; he was aware of his heart beating, of the weight of his head on his forearm and had a sense, for a second, that his right arm was somehow different from his left, that they were two mutually incompatible limbs; he kept his left leg stretched out and drew in the right one, bending his knee and resting the sole of his foot on the ground. Lying in this position, with his eyes tight shut, he had the momentary illusion that his limbs would no longer obey him if, for example, he were to decide to get up and walk over to the wood or choose perhaps to raise his arms or cross them or place his hands near his waist on his hips, between sword belt and skin. He stretched out his right leg and removed his arm so that his head was resting on the sand, then extended his right arm so that it lay in exactly the same position as his left, at an angle of sixty degrees to his body, palms uppermost; then he lay there absolutely still. He felt that he could actually hear the water evaporating and his skin growing warm, toasting in the sun's rays, a dull, barely audible creaking similar to the noise he thought he had heard before in the gradual relaxation of pores and sphincters. He did not go to sleep at once, only very gradually, and then barely slept. It was more as if, in the most complete silence, in the digressive zone of his mind (small in comparison to the zone of darkness), he was feeling and seeing a returning procession of cities long dead, whose stones floated by, then disappeared, or a procession of vanished faces that surfaced for a moment only to dissolve at once into yellow smoke, lacking the permanence that might prove their former reality. Then came the empty sky. With obdurate calm, the captain bore this stasis, but only for a matter of moments, then he opened his eyes, stood up and stretched. He thought: "Now I'm going to turn round, walk over to the wood and see if I feel again that recollection of having known it before I ever came here." With long, measured strides he approached the line of low, dusty trees behind which the small wood huddled, tangled and knotted, a frozen tumult of creepers and lianas; as he did so he observed how the trees seemed to grow in size or advance towards him. The recollection came back to him at once, when he had barely set foot on the grey carpet of dead leaves that scrunched and cracked beneath his boots, but again, as on the first occasion, it came alone, without the object it recollected, as if the possibility of the recollection existed, but lacked a reality to attach it to. The captain strolled amongst the murmuring leaves, his arms folded across his bare chest, and walked the whole length of the semicircle of trees, passing the point where they grew nearest to the fort and then leaving it behind as he approached the farther end; then he went back to where he had started from and leaned against a tree, looking at what lay before him: the opposite end of the wood, the fort with its stockade of pointed sticks, the half-ruined straw and adobe huts and the expanse of sandy soil sloping down to the river; above were the high, glittering sun and the blue, empty sky. The captain's sun-scorched face was washed clean and his hair and beard were growing curly again as they dried. His dark eyes were half closed, intent, studying the scene. Then he shook his head, gave a short laugh and, followed now by only the briefest of shadows, walked back towards the fort.

When he went in, he walked over to the priest and crouched down beside him. He was dead. With vacant curiosity the captain looked at the dead face, at the dead eyes, blind and white, as opaque as if made of stone. A fly buzzed around the priest. The captain made no attempt to brush it away: he watched it hover, buzz and land on one corner of the dead mouth, then take off, buzz and land again. He was just about to curse the priest when he sensed something was wrong; looking up, he saw that the redheaded soldier had gone. He jumped to his feet and looked calmly around him: he saw only the corpses and the huts, all completely silent. The captain called out.

"Judas!" he said, "Judas!"

In the empty air his voice sounded strange, slow and hoarse. He took a couple of paces, stepped over the priest's body, then paused again. "Judas!" he said and looked at the one hut that was still intact. "Come out of there. I know you're in there. Drag yourself out here like the red snake you are; I'll cut you into little pieces when I get hold of you."

Skirting or striding over the corpses, the captain walked on in the utter silence towards the hut. His washed-clean face was once more damp with sweat and, though his eyes seemed to smile, his jaws were clenched. "Come out of there now and don't make me lose my temper," he said, as he approached the hut. "I'll give you quince jelly and wine and I'll be nice to you even though your father was Judas and your mother was a whore. You're a rogue and a scoundrel but I know you're frightened and half-crazy so I won't harm you."

The captain advanced towards the hut, whose rough adobe walls refracted the sun's rays. The vertical hole that served as the door formed a black rectangle.

"Come out, you devil's fart, and tell me all those stories you made up. Come out right now or else make the sign of the cross and commend your soul to God." The captain, still moving forwards, laughed as he said this.

When he reached the hut he stopped and leaned against the doorway. At first he could see nothing but darkness inside. Then his momentary blindness cleared — he blinked for a moment — and he saw the redheaded soldier sitting on a large chest, his seemingly non-existent legs hanging down, his back leaning against the wall and an arquebus in his hands aimed straight at the captain's head.

"You've got to give them a Christian burial, captain," said the soldier.

The captain roared with laughter. When the laughter stopped he looked at the soldier.

"I'll give *you* a Christian burial, once I've torn you to shreds," he said.

"Go and give them a Christian burial and the devil will leave you," said the soldier.

His voice was very calm. The captain looked at him with rancorous eyes.

"Come on, blabbermouth," he murmured, "tell me about the king and about Madrid. Tell me, I'll believe anything you say."

The soldier said: "If you go out into the courtyard, captain, and pick up the spade that's out there and start digging, the devil inside will leave you. Go on. I'll be in here listening."

The captain took one step forward and stopped.

"Out of my way," he said.

"One more step, captain, and I'll shoot," said the soldier.

"Just let me get the quince jelly out of that chest, I'll give you a slice," said the captain.

Now he could clearly make out the interior of the hut. The soldier was alert, watching him.

"Go and give them a decent burial," he said.

The captain stroked his beard, shaking his head.

"You red devil," he said, lunging forward; his voice was drowned by the explosion.

Translated by Margaret Jull Costa

Five Hundred Years Ago

Daniel Moyano

*H*e was outside the village cutting branches for his new home but everything he was hearing, all that was happening, told him his efforts no longer made sense. It was useless for him to chop the branches — he was trying to prolong something that was slipping away, had already become part of the past. His companions were telling him that the invaders had finally landed. The newcomers brought with them unimaginable weapons and ferocious animals, and the villagers had decided to surrender everything in return for their lives. They had been counted and shared out, and so had he, even though the newcomers had not seen him; not even his wife or son fully belonged to him any more. So what he was doing was senseless, all he could do was return to the village and give himself up like everyone else.

Each word his companions added about the new situation robbed his existence of a little more of its truth, took over yet another part of what until then he had understood by reality. That reality, yielding to the new meaning, was vanishing bit by bit, leaving only emptiness — immediately filled by the fear that shone in his wife's eyes as she dropped the useless bundle of branches she had been carrying. The world had suddenly been turned upside down for everyone except his young son. Absorbed in his task, the boy went on cutting fresh shoots, the kind used to bind the tougher ones together, while yellow traces of the ostrich egg he had eaten before leaving the village dried round his mouth.

The sunny morning air turned suddenly cold, chilled by his companions' terrible words, which engulfed him, pierced his body like a curse. Even though he shut himself off to try to stop them, even though he put his hands over his ears, they penetrated skin and bone, grew and grew inside him until he was a different person, while the task he had still to finish receded for ever into the past.

Since childhood he had heard that some men like gods would come, perhaps from the air, to take them all off to an ill-defined paradise. But that would be after many moons had passed. Now those moons had gone by, and time was at an end. Had these newcomers flown to the village? he asked, without looking at anyone. No, but they might be capable of it; and his friends showed him a mirror that they had brought, proof of their power. It reflected his face like the river did, but there was no movement: time really had come to a stop.

The invaders owned many things like that, the words said, as his companions used signs to describe dogs and horses, wheels and arquebuses, possible attributes of the predicted heaven. Many? he asked, referring to those who had resisted and died, and the reply was a wail of confirmation: many. If they have killed they cannot come from heaven, he thought as they crossed the river close by the captured village, and for the first time in his world heard the barking of dogs. He shuddered as his friends explained that they were like weapons, but were living beings.

He had not yet seen the invading gods, but he could feel their presence. Everything around him had changed. It was as if they had felled the trees, even though they still stood upright. The wild animals in the woods and rivers also belonged to them, had most likely been counted and shared out as well. The power of these men gods existed in its own right, they did not need to be there for him to be aware of it. Without even appearing, their terrible truth had reached the hut he had been building out beyond the village, in a place they might never see but which now was theirs. This is what he was thinking, or what someone else was thinking for him. The thoughts came from somewhere outside, no longer seemed to be his.

Without the words to describe them, he saw them. Dogs and

horses were tied like monstrous nightmares to the trees he knew so well. Armed men had surrounded the village, guarding the site that must surely no longer be sacred. They had pillaged everything in their search for shiny metals, even the funeral urns. And as they rushed about, they screeched in a language from another world, a language that must be a close relative of the harsh barking of the arquebuses, which brought instant death.

He crept into his village like an intruder and gave himself up. He did not dare look his guard in the face: he stared at his boots, up as far as the pommel of his sword. By his words and actions, his guard showed he could perform deeds denied to his prisoner. The weapons proved that all that he could do in this new situation was at the will of his guard, whose reality annulled his own. Of the two of them, only the other existed.

With the setting of the sun, the noise and haste began. There were shouts of command, then they had to run through the darkness, prodded by the arquebuses. They had to lift loads, carry them through the forest to the cries of the night birds, birds of ill-omen, while the wild animals fled the clanking iron, the swords slashing at the undergrowth to reveal a moon that started the dogs howling. A horse brushed past him but did not bite. He thought: it does not speak yet it is not fierce; then with the first light of dawn he could hear the distant rumour of the sea that separates the living from the dead.

From the rowing-boat he saw the galleon, its floating wings folded on the sea, just waiting for them to arrive before flying off again. He felt he was living a very precise moment in which both land and sea were completely still, outside time. One of the men thrust an oar into the edge of the earth. He was so strong he pushed it away. The sea stayed calm but the earth began to slide backwards. Everything he knew was drifting away: the shore, beyond it the jungle with its jaguars and birds; the village and the funeral urns the invaders had not dug up, the seasons for hunting and for fruits, grinding the maize and for the birth of children: everything was being left behind, pushed away by the god's oar. He felt under his tunic for the green stone arrowhead, the amulet and the clay pipe his wife had given him when they first slept together. All that was left to take with him to the other world.

The ship was not a huge hollowed-out tree. It was thousands of trees chopped and shaped together to make a great hollow that floated. The newcomers climbed effortlessly up the rope between the boat and the galleon, but his own legs froze. Two men, whose eyes he saw for the first time and who seemed not so cruel, lifted him as though his body was weightless. The world he was leaving behind seemed to fly backwards. The great trees of the coast dwindled to the size of a maize stem. His companions may have been on the shore, slipping away with the land, but they were too small to be seen, let alone his little boy, mouth stained yellow with the remains of the ostrich egg.

Tied to a post, he could see the astonishment on the faces of the men who came out of the depths of the ship to stare at him. Not all of them had metallic heads or long beards. Some seemed as ordinary as him. He saw sick faces, sunken eyes, hands calloused from working ropes and sails, gentle, sad gazes.

These were the ones who shouted and swarmed round the ropes and sails when the waves of the sea, furious at the wind, swelled up like blisters. They ran from side to side in response to commands, gathered the sails on their posts, and the wind and the men shrieked as if speaking the same tongue.

The ship allowed the sea to run through it, while the land sailed off in the distance, with its rivers and mountains, clouds and condors, his son and the warmth of his wife's body. The sea which he now saw in tiny portions, seeping through the bottom of the galleon, in the bucket he had to use to try to capture it and throw it back into the sea.

The galleon, which was pure make-believe. The truth was the rivers and beasts he remembered, women and animals giving birth, the living and the dead. Everything around him now was a violent balancing act, something that had been constructed and was only barely held together by a precarious mechanism. If the bucket did not keep emptying out the water that seeped in through the holes, everything would sink without trace. If the trees so laboriously shaped and bound became untied and went back to being trees, the galleon would take all these phantoms with it to the bottom of the sea: men, dogs, horses, arquebuses and their fire. The sea was not natural like rain. No one could live on it, not even birds. Those who defied it were not of this world: they were either gods or the dead, headed for a meaningless paradise.

The stars had changed too; the ones he knew had disappeared with the land when the oar pushed it away. To keep his mind free from the exhausting tasks they imposed on him, he clung to the fact that at least there was no change in the succession of light and darkness, or of sleep and waking. That was all he could be sure of. They had not been able to change these things by tying them with ropes or chains, to kill them with arquebuses or tear at them with their dogs. All the rest was an invention which could come crashing down at any moment of its own accord, when the dream had outlasted itself: pure invention this journey, the metals they covered their heads with, the fire from their weapons, pure invention their incomprehensible words, their mirrors and papers, their ships with cloths draped in the wind, invention their beards and their shouts, their cruelty and their silence. What would his boy, who stood scarcely higher than the ground, be doing at this moment? Who was protecting him from the bad weather and the wild animals in the forest? Was there still a bloom on his wife's skin, where had the wind blown his roof branches? All that had been drained of its reality as well, it was all so far off, pushed away by the tip of the oar. It must be true then that he was crossing the sea, or the sea was crossing him, in a way unthinkable for anyone in this life. He must be travelling to the paradise where the forefathers went to smoke their pipes for all eternity, he must be as unreal as those taking him to this unknown destination.

At night, tiny living beings shared his corner with him. Their scuttling movements sometimes coincided with the men's, but the creatures were so quick they almost always escaped their boots. When they did not, their dark-coloured shells burst underfoot with the sound of dried fruit being crushed by stones. These beings had no blood, only a trickle of liquid that was soon absorbed by the wooden planks. There were other, bigger creatures which gnawed at the wood too, devouring the ship bite after bite, but whenever anyone came near, they vanished. All he had seen of them were their tiny gleaming eyes, and the occasional flash of a shiny ashen tail. They lived on whatever scraps of food they could find, and at night seemed to be in charge of the ship.

Men and ship, stars and suns, were all enclosed by the sea. And the sea was not water. Water was what came from rivers. The sea was space, was this sense of waiting with nothing behind or in front. It would not let him be himself or have memories. It contained everything at the same time as it overflowed everywhere. Even if they collected a thousand galleons like the one he was in, with a thousand men in each, the sea would always be alone. It would not allow company of any kind. It was no more than its colour, its noise and its foam. It was what was behind all things, the father of everything, the beginning. And these men were part of the sea. He had seen them run crazily across the deck when storms arose. They cursed the sea, they did not fear it. They and their arquebuses understood the language of the storms. They were all of the same tribe. In their shouting, they themselves became arquebuses firing at the storms.

If the sea was the path taken by the dead forefathers, and never came to an end, that must mean the dead never reached their destination. To die meant to be travelling for ever, or to be stuck in one place while the earth went spinning further and further away with no possibility of return. If the sea did come to an end somewhere, they must be on their way to paradise. The sun rose and set within the sea, so the sea must also contain the paradise he had been told of. The earth and all notion of it had disappeared. He looked up at the wind swelling the sails and knew inside himself that he was on the way to that place where there was no cold, no illnesses, where for each fruit picked from a tree a fresh one appeared symmetrically, where you lived for ever because you were on a never-ending journey.

The men sang and drank, accompanying themselves on a piece of musical wood. They also gave him some of the purple liquid, then put the piece of wood in his hands. It was shaped like a woman and had many strings. He could play on one of them which contained sounds he knew and others he had never heard. He began to sing. The men listened to him, swaying their heads and clinking their cups. In his song he thanked them for the drink and asked them where they, the horses and the dogs all came from, who had given them the arquebuses and the galleon, where they were taking him, why they had killed, what would happen to those of his tribe left behind, guarded by more people like them. When he finished, they patted his back in a friendly way, and that night let him sleep untied. The sounds of the musical wood continued late into the night, and dissolved with him into sleep.

He woke as always clutching the objects he had brought from his world, which still connected him to his former existence. The ship was quiet, serene. So was the sea, which at last had ended. Dulled by amazement, he stared in disbelief at a mass of lines and curves made solid: the lofty towers and spires of paradise.

The houses of this discovered heaven seemed to float in the air, but their stones were firmly rooted in the ground, which was a reddish, porous earth that looked freshly ploughed. Dogs and horses glided through the grass as if in a dream; the same dream contained the trees that the galleons had been made from. There were birds too, as in his world. Paradise revealed itself to him slowly, not keeping pace with his anxious desire to see its full extent in one long look. The land was not level, but rose and fell in a way that prevented him seeing it all. The people in the villages stood in their doorways to watch the soldiers pass by; they all stared at him, at the feathers on his head and the parrot he was carrying in a cage. The sun had risen high in the sky from the distant sea. So paradise was not in the other world, or if it was, the sun was the same for death as for life.

Over a river he saw some stones shaped so that they were suspended above the water with almost no support, which meant the dwellers in paradise could ford the river without using canoes or getting their feet wet. Those same trees that he had seen doubled to make the galleons were here bent until the tips of their trunks met without breaking, and joined with other wooden struts like stars. When they were pulled along by horses, they turned on themselves, and people and things were carried from place to place on them.

He walked alongside a horse, staring at its lathered flanks and the soldier's boots. He understood that the animal was gentle, not the kind to use swords or arquebuses. An animal like all the others, and a fine one too. He spoke to it in friendship. He saw its ears twitch, to show that it was listening. The soldier laughed.

From the tallest house in one village, topped off like a tower, he could hear the sound of bells. He heard the sound die away until the red-roofed village and its curious inhabitants had disappeared behind another rise. Men, carriages and horses flowed like waves over the surface of paradise, sweeping past villages that peered out then disappeared.

He thought that the faces of the people here were not different as they were in his world. They all looked the same, with the same fixed smile or profile. Thousands of identical faces gazed at him in astonishment. In the mirror they gave him, he looked again at his own face and saw it was not like theirs. It was a different colour, had different lips, and he was wearing the feathers they had forced him to put on even though it was not the right time. He saw he was half-naked. Thousands of copies of the same face, flattened, reproduced, stared at him and the parrot with the same interest. Suddenly, he felt ashamed. He was a monster, disturbing the harmony of this carefully cultivated and decorated paradise.

In every village the tallest house had a tower of bells. All identical, like the faces of the people. Their convoy stopped in front of one of them, and the leaders of the soldiers went in. An ear-splitting music, thousands of enormous flutes blown in unison, came from inside, then a murmur of voices like the sound of rivers at night. Faces went past, staring at him and the parrot. The soldier and his arquebus, which was powerful here too, would not allow them to come too near. There were old men in rags who stretched out their hands to the soldiers and the people in fine clothes going into this house: and lots of barefoot children who did the same, begging; men and women displaying objects or food while they shouted something desperately sad, like the plaintive cry of a distant bird high over the forest. Tame dogs, little grey horses and woollen animals were all mixed in with the people wailing; the voices inside the house also sounded like the call of wild birds, a sound of weeping; then the soldiers left the building and there were more bells, equally sad.

His guards let a man wrapped in black clothes come closer than he should have to talk to him, trying to translate what he was saying with repeated gestures. Then the man gave him a picture showing a beautiful woman holding a baby in her arms. He guessed intuitively that the woman and child in the picture must live in the house they had all visited.

There were shouts for them to move on. A woman carrying a jug of water asked the soldier if she could approach him. She came so close she could almost touch him, and stared intently at him with her deep green eyes while he drank. He hurried to store that look inside himself: it was like a precious green stone found at the bottom of a pit. He also stored away the fragrance of herbs on the woman, still staring at him with the amazing sweep of green sea that he saw in her eyes. The carts moved off, the soldier pushed him on his way, and the green-eyed woman walked off, but when they reached the summit of the next hill and the village disappeared from view, he could still see two green dots twinkling in the sky like a snake bite.

He walked carefully, as if he were still being watched by the eyes that had looked at him. He knew that all the good things on this earth were beautiful because the gods looked on them when they created them. He could feel the breeze from the hills lingering round his near-naked body, sensed that his silhouette stood out proud in the wind. The dogs and horses were no longer ferocious, and after the village had disappeared he sniffed at his arms and hands; the fragrance of herbs was still there; he smelt of them, of her.

They had travelled a long way into paradise when an endless rainstorm gave him the chance to consider all he had seen. This must be paradise, but then why were there dogs? And what about the beggars, the punishments, the men in black in their houses full of bells and wailing, what about the rich in their carriages, the blind people, the arquebuses and daggers? The galleons stayed afloat by miracle; what if the circled wood of the cartwheels suddenly straightened out to return to its original shape? Then the wheels would become branches again, and would let everything plunge into the precipice. These madmen could lose everything in an instant. Horses and arquebuses could rebel and turn against them. They had artificially built up a world that could fall to pieces with a moment's carelessness. Why were there so many beggars: where could they all find food? These men lived together but punished each other, there were clubs and knives and defenceless people; and nearly every face wore a sad expression — that was the grin that made them all look identical; everything was on the verge of collapse, of death; beautiful bodies hidden under clothes as if they were ashamed of being alive. Where were the gods, if everything was as sad as the sound of their bells? These clothed people who never seemed to be happy, everything was so serious in paradise: no one could look at anyone else's body or even at their own; sad the body that was never at play; everywhere piling broken trees on cut stone to make houses and bells and huge doors for temples where they shut in their wailing and their fear; bells and arquebuses, beggars and clubs. Someone was crying outside in the night rain. The rains of paradise were sad, and everyone was all alone, however much they mixed stones and wood and metal, however much they sailed, begged, meted out punishment, stood guard, prayed, hid the beauty of their bodies as if they were scared of it. They cried in the rain, they were gods who had no gods, they spent their whole time building up this paradise but it was always crumbling around them; if they allowed themselves to be happy for a single moment, it would all come crashing down: houses, towers, leaders, horses, beggars.

Screeching like the galleons tossed by storm winds, thousands of servants and soldiers swarmed around, cleaning the streets and monuments, chasing off the beggars, laying brand new carpets between the street and the huge palace lit up for the arrival of the great leader, whose carriage of stars was approaching.

He stepped out of his coach surrounded by a thousand guards, entered the palace where a thousand candles greeted him. The leader sat on the throne, and soldiers came to fetch him and his parrot, stuck the meaningless feathers on his head, showed him how he should behave when he was in the august presence.

Men in magnificent garments stood close by — but not too close — to the leader high on his golden throne, wearing a crown with stones like huge solidified tears. He was one living jewel, and the palace a larger one. But if this man were to lift just one hand in anger, the whole palace would vanish. Everything in paradise, all the people and towns from the sea to here, knelt fearfully around him at their centre. The galleons were the rims of this leader's garments, so was the sea; the hut he did not have the time to finish in his village was a hidden thread in the border of his cloak decorated with nascent pearls, the beggars driven off were his fleas.

A soldier instructed him to advance slowly with his cage. He took a few steps then bowed as they had shown him. He saw that the chief in the glittering robe had turned his fish eyes on him and his parrot. When someone pushed up his hand with the parrot for the leader to see it better, he sneaked a look at the whey-coloured face. The eyes expressed neither good nor bad, but reminded him only of a dead fish. All the jewels, the gold, the tapestries, the lights and the distant cities clustered round these lifeless eyes, the centre, the heart of paradise.

He went back to his place with the cage. He had been told to stand there without moving until he was dismissed. Blasts of music were the signal for the leader in the cape to rise; he left the palace and climbed back into his coach with its blue horses. The servants rolled up the carpet in the street, snuffed out all the candles. As the coach moved off, all the windows in the street burst open again, people appeared, the beggars returned, night fell.

The galleons had been to his village to fetch what little precious metal they could find there. Some tiny nuggets of gold that would gleam unnoticed among all these lights and pearls. He was beginning to understand. He was still standing where they had told him to wait, certain that by staying there motionless he was helping to hold up the weight of this paradise. He remembered he was not to move until he was told to. If he did, a wheel might spring straight, or one of the towers with bells crash to the ground. So he stayed on the spot, doing his bit to keep the palace and all the rest in place. He did not even dare push away a feather tickling his nose.

The man dressed in black sprinkled water on his head, drew lines in the air and called him José. His guard, whose lands he was to work, slapped him on the back and also called him by the new name. Using signs, he indicated that he was no longer an animal, but a human being like him and everyone else in paradise. The true God would protect him for ever — he could see the God on the church altar if he wished. There was gold there too, and paintings that seemed alive, long tall columns, and closed-in windows that changed the colour of the sun. He looked for his God among the many he could see. There were some with wings who looked like children, beautiful little boys and girls. The guard pushed him to face the altar. His god was nailed to two crossed planks of wood, hanging down with a wound in his side, from which blood trickled without moving. It's impossible, he said in his own language, but his guard's finger continued to point at the prostrate god. But he's dead, he said, and tried to say more, but the words, silenced by fear, refused to come out.

He wanted to ask who had killed the god and why, perhaps it was those ferocious dogs. His guard was making a cross on his face and chest. The people were praying because they knew they were going to die; just like their god, they would have a wound in their side. His own knees were trembling, he was afraid, with the fear he had seen on his wife's face when the newcomers had arrived in the village. He realized that once he had been sprinkled with water he too was bound to die, they would nail him to two wooden planks as they had done to their god. In his village, death was a door that opened; here, it closed for ever. That was why the people here were always sad, why there were arquebuses and dogs; that was why they covered their bodies and could never be lighthearted. That was why they were busy all the time shoring up their paradise: in order to forget death. The old people, in his own land, did not die like this: they simply moved on. But now he, with his new name, would be left on a cross to die. That was what was wrong in paradise: instead of opening a door, death shut it.

As he left the church he could feel this death taking possession of him, accompanying him and his shadow along the street. The beggars stared at him with dying eyes; the fish eyes of the great lord in the cape had glimpsed death behind the jewels and the lights; the galleons had crossed the seas in search of embellishments for death — he could see the shiny metal everywhere in this paradise. His legs were aching from having to carry death like this, with his name José. He clutched at the few objects in his pocket that he had brought from home. They at least were still alive.

Today you do not have to work, his guard told him, warning him to return before sunset. One day was a very small amount of time for him, accustomed as he was to measuring it by the moon or the harvest. Here they chopped time up into days, so that real time was lost for everyone. Even so, this was his first free day in paradise: he could rest until nightfall, or go wherever he wished. Perhaps it would be good just to wander through the green fields under the newly risen sun, but to head in that direction meant he would have to tread on his shadow, which was not right on a day like this. He chose instead to walk towards the sun as it climbed the sky, towards the city he had passed through, whose spires and towers he could already see at the top of a hill.

Groans of misery led him to an enclosed square along the sides of which thousands of people were sitting on wooden planks staring at a huge bonfire. To him it looked like a ship, or the church where he was given his name, except that here the gods were alive, made of flesh and blood just like him. The greatest of them sat under an awning. He was not nailed to a cross, but held a tiny one in his hands. The glow from the flames lit up the god's face, a mixture of piety, cruelty and madness. Some men, their hands tied behind their backs and hoods on their heads, were driven out of pits by soldiers on horseback. They were paraded before the god under his awning, who shouted out "heretic!" and brandished his cross. The horses, seemingly as furious at the word as the soldiers who rode them, pushed the men towards the bonfire, while that one word hung in the air, circling round and round the silent heads peering out of windows into this huge ship.

He was about to run away, but everywhere around him beggars were rushing to join in the spectacle of fire. He tried to concentrate his mind, to see if he could save the victims waiting to be called "heretics!" and thrown on the fire, and the others already leaving the pits. He wished that all the pieces of wood in paradise would spring free and return to their natural state as trees; he wished the platform and the awning would collapse under the gods who were ordering the burning; he wished that all the trunks twisted so painfully to make wheels would change back to trees there and then, covering the square in a forest; he wished that all the horses and dogs would turn against these living gods who were passing sentence on other animals; he wished the rain would come to drown the fire, that this invented paradise would collapse for ever.

He waited and waited. His desire was so intense he thought it was bound to happen. But the wooden planks refused to budge, would not dislodge the nails driven into them; the stench of smoke, burning clothes and flesh smeared the clear sky.

It was the turn of two small figures in hoods, tied to a length of rope pulled by a soldier, to hear the word "heretics!" It circled with the dying echoes of the earlier one, the two words hovering above the crowd like two black winged birds of prey. After the sentence had been read, a priest spoke some words of consolation to the pair, who immediately started screaming so loudly that the horses reared up in fright; the man called José knew their screams had taken this paradise a step closer to the hell the priests so often talked of.

A soldier gently removed the couple's hoods and their clothes. One of them was female. Cover their shame, a voice called out; then their fine bodies, with their shame covered, were tied to posts that would be consumed with them. Their screams in the flames were shortlived, as if the sounds too were being burned, robbed of the strength to climb to the heights where "heretics!" was still circling. Under the soldiers, the horses struggled to contain their fear; José could tell without pressing his ear to their flanks that their hearts were beating wildly.

There were pauses between the executions for papers to be read and signed, delays that were almost as unbearable as the burnings themselves, stretching one death out into the next one; in the silences, the very existence of this paradise seemed to hang in doubt.

The heretics and the kindly priest waited; the living gods up on their platform, their flickering shadows thrown onto the walls of the square by the flames, waited breathless during this pause in the mechanism that drove on all the killings; all the villages of paradise seemed to be waiting too, and the galleons on the sea. All of this to make death more certain.

Now the pause came to an end: the good priest whispered in

the ear of fresh victims; one soldier stripped them, another set light to the fire under them. The flames gleamed in miniature in the eyes of onlookers and horses; on the distant seas, the galleons sank not a fraction of an inch; although it is so fragile, the wheels of paradise continued to turn. There was someone to perform every function: gods and jailers, interrogators and prosecutors, beggars and soldiers, all of them keeping the machinery in motion. The arquebuses and horses were their attributes, as they all clustered around the gold that would not let them sleep, around the flames that were like liquid gold melting into the sky.

The flames stifled words more quickly than bodies, but some did escape, manage to survive longer than the others to make sense to José's ears. "Ay, God have mercy on my soul," he heard, and stored it away inside him together with the green look of the woman who had offered him a drink; two things he would take with him from paradise if ever he escaped.

All this was happening, he thought, because the god they worshipped was dead, and because of things like wheels, arquebuses and dogs, because of bridges and bells. The living gods who dictated the sentences, the beggars and the people watching had all come to see variations of the death they worshipped on the cross inside the church, a death which today was roaming free like him. They constructed death as they did their ships, destroying people as they did trees. He sensed that the name he had been given made him part of the framework of this death: he could feel it rising up along his legs, while the name that had been his in his village slipped away from him. It no longer made sense. Who could remember it, now he was José? He could be condemned to death as a heretic, José who should have been back at his master's house before sunset, which had come and gone.

The name was crawling up inside him, searching for a way out, painful as though it were burning him. He wanted to get back, to beg his master to bind his body so tight that the word could not reach his heart. He thought that if the dead god had been alive and could see all this, he would shout out on his wooden planks: "Ay, God have mercy on my body," he would have said before being burnt to ashes on his cross.

A choking sensation told him the name had reached his lungs. He struggled to push his way through the crowd and out of the square. Now all of him was José, he could feel the word coursing through his blood. All the memories of his own land were being consumed in a secret fire. Night had fallen. He had reached the top of the hill, and could see the lights of his master's house in the distance. His master, the same man who had guarded him on board ship, who had given him the purple liquid which had cheered his spirits. He would beg his master to bind him as tightly as if he had a snake bite, to stop this unbearable sadness he could not name throbbing in his veins like a poison.

He tried to call out to his master, but the words were stifled by the name José that had taken him over completely. He stumbled down the hill, desperate to reach the distant light, then fell over in some spot or other of this endless paradise.

With the last of his free day, the last of his life, he raised a hand to his mouth to wipe away a thin trickle of saliva or blood that for a second reminded him of the stain from an ostrich egg. The yellow fleck disappeared into the morass of death while paradise sailed steadfastly on with its precarious structure of stones and cruelty, bells and madness, sailed on to its unknown destination.

Translated by Nick Caistor

Pateco's Little Prank

Ana Lydia Vega

Black José Clemente
fell hopelessly in love
on the River Plata
with mulatto María Laó
Puerto Rican folklore

Papá Ogún, god of war,
boots black as pitch
and when he walks
the earth trembles . . .
Luis Palés Matos

*T*he Monteros were the masters of a prosperous sugar-cane plantation. Twenty-five black slaves worked themselves to death from sunup to sundown to fatten the bellies and the purses of the family. The enormous house of the Monteros rose up ever higher, whiter and prouder over the tassels of the cane fields.

Pateco Patadecabro, always a mischievous prankster, wanted to play a big joke on the Monteros. And with the approval of the African gods, he stuck his cloven goat's hoof in India ink, powdered it with wheat flour and sang in a tuneless voice:

Stride and sack
Sack and stride
White and black
Black and white

"Get that monster out of here!", bellowed Doña Amalia Montero, turning pale at the sight of that thing which, after nine months of misery, was kicking happily at her side. And she became whiter than Snow White when the midwife assured her that indeed her legitimate and long-awaited firstborn, through one of life's mysterious tricks, had been born with a white body and a black head.

Needless to say, the mother refused to believe it. What

possible relation could this two-colour beast have to her lily-white flesh, golden tresses and bluer-than-blue blood inherited from Old Castile? What would the aristocratic ladies and distinguished gentlemen of pure European lineage say at the christening of this very exotic newborn?

The fat rat of doubt gnawed tirelessly away at the heart of Don Felipe Montero. One rainy night, he ordered Cristóbal, one of the slaves, to take the incriminating infant and abandon it on to the mountain to the mercy of the elements.

But Cristóbal, as usually happens in such cases, took pity on the child and saved its life, leaving it in the care of a healing woman named Mamá Ochú.

Mamá Ochú lived in a humble little shack on the banks of the River Plata. There she took charge of the baby, nursed him and dressed him as well as she could in her poverty. As soon as the child was old enough to understand, his guardian said to him:

"You will be called José Clemente. And you will not leave this house without my permission. Outside these walls, evil roams."

Enclosed in the shack, ignorant of the world, José Clemente watched the days pass without distinguishing them from the nights. The stories Mamá Ochú told him — stories of Pateco, Calconte and the Great Beast, of Juan Calalú and the Princess Moriviví — were his only distraction.

But soon the child's curiosity and thirst for life had grown such that one day he asked the old *curandera*, very respectfully:

"Why am I white and you black, Mamá Ochú?"

Frightened, Mamá Ochú crossed herself three times and once in reverse. There were no mirrors in the house and the child, who had seen only his body and not his head, believed in his absolute whiteness. Mamá Ochú didn't know how to tell him the truth, and to avoid causing him pain she burst out, "Because that was the will of the Almighty Lord Changó."

The child seemed to be content with that explanation. Perhaps he was. Time went by and Mamá Ochú went along secure in the belief that the storm had passed, until one day it circled back with renewed force:

"Mamá Ochú, what colour are my eyes?"

"Blue as the river," lied the poor old woman, asking Changó's forgiveness for such a sacrilege.

"And my hair, Mamá Ochú?"

"Yellow as the sun."

That was when José Clemente truly began to wish to meet the river, to know the sun and to discover his own face. But his guardian reminded him that evil walked freely in the countryside, and the poor little thing continued to ferment fantasies in the still of his clandestine dreams.

The years galloped by. José Clemente was a tall, strong boy. His curiosity had grown with his body. One day when Mamá Ochú was out-and-about looking for wood for the fire, a very suspicious gust of wind suddenly opened the window. And the world, the river and the sun were born.

And something else. Because in that blessed instant, as if by coincidence, a young slave girl chanced to pass by. She was a girl of such bewitching beauty that she would have made Temban-dumba of far-away Quimbamba burst with envy. She was coming to bathe in the river and was about to take off her petticoat and camisole when José Clemente, who was struck stupid at the sight of her, asked innocently:

"Are you the Princess Morivíví?"

Seeing the black head on the white body framed in the window, María Laó — for the beauty was graced with that name — was so frightened that she turned and ran, thinking that she had encountered that very devil Pateco, or something far worse.

Without a moment's hesitation, José Clemente jumped down from the window and pursued her for a stretch but, lighter than a kite in March, the girl disappeared.

In an agony of love, José Clemente threw himself down to cry next to the river. That was how he came to see himself for the first time. That was how he learned that he had neither blue eyes nor yellow hair. And he cried even more bitterly. He cried so much and so long that the river rose. The waters churned in an unexpected whirlpool and from them surged the big, strong, black body of Ogún, wrapped in a wave of fire, with the red bandana on his head and the machete shining at his waist.

"Don't cry, José Clemente," said the apparition in a booming voice.

The boy fell on all fours. Mamá Ochú had taught him to respect his elders and his gods. He didn't dare to even lift his head from the ground.

"Ogún is not pleased with tears," thundered the vision. "Stop crying!"

"Oh, Papá Ogún!", whimpered José Clemente. "Look how unfortunate I am. Help me to find the Princess Moriviví."

Ogún let out a burst of laughter that shook the mountains of the Central Range.

"This is not a land of princesses," he said, his belly swollen with laughter.

"Then at least return my colour," said the boy, blushing a little in the face of Ogún's ridicule.

The god became serious, and then he resounded as sharply as taut leather:

> Your true colour
> is among your own.
> You will not be two
> when you are one.

And handing the boy his machete, he faded away back to where he had come from.

José Clemente was left pensive. What had Ogún meant? Mamá Ochú had told him that the gods spoke in riddles.

He got up and set out walking through the countryside. He didn't know what to do or where to go. While he wandered through the leaves and the stalks of cane, night fell. The owls watched him with surprise from the branches of the mango tree. The bats grazed by him as he blindly walked on.

Suddenly, a reddish brightness closed his eyes. The smell of burnt cane took the air by surprise. A scene of blazing cane fields

opened like a lake of fire before the timid gaze of José Clemente.
The flames were hungrily licking the dark sky.

Screams were heard in the distance. José Clemente broke into
a run, struggling against the smoke. When he arrived at the place
where the cries seemed to be coming from, he saw the great,
sprawling manor house being devoured by flames. In one of the
windows, two pairs of white arms waved like savage fans. The
cries for help were deafening.

At the same time, other moans wounded the boy's ears. They
came half-smothered from a miserable slave barracks that was
also on fire.

Indecision squatted on his brow like a bad-tempered wash
woman. To help the occupants of the big white house first. Or to
help those in the barracks first. This thing was harder than
cracking boiling *lerenes* with your teeth. Mamá Ochú always said:
do good and don't notice for whom. Only now there were two
somebodies to not notice. José Clemente closed his eyes,
breathed deeply, put his fingers together and called with all his
might to Papá Ogún. The sneering crackle of the fire silenced his
invocation.

From both sides, the cries and laments were growing more
desperate. As if moved by a greater power, José Clemente
headed toward the barracks. There the trapped men and women
were pounding the boards with scarred hands. There too, María
Laó pulled bravely at her father's shackles, searching for a way
out. A single blow of Ogún's machete shattered the chains and
let everyone go free, as it should be. Facing the flames, they all
undertook the hurried journey into the darkness. The big white
house was still burning like a bonfire in the night.

With the happy group of freed slaves following his steps, José
Clemente lost himself once more in the underbush. At daybreak,
without intending to, he found himself once again in front of
Mamá Ochú's little shack. The kind old woman waited for her
protégé next to the river, praying to Changó, Orula, Obatalá
and any other divinity that came to mind. Imagine her surprise at

seeing the boy, machete in hand, followed by his people, with his body as black as his head and a fugitive smile on his lips.

"Praise be to Changó, and to Papá Ogún, his valiant warrior!", said Mamá Ochú, crying with happiness on hearing the story told by the new arrival.

And that was how Pateco punished the Monteros. José Clemente regained his true colour, while the great house and sugar-mill were consumed by the fire of Ogún.

Translated by Carol J. Wallace

Chac Mool

Carlos Fuentes

Not long ago, Filiberto was drowned at Acapulco. It happened at Easter. Despite having lost his job at the Ministry, he could not resist the bureaucratic pull of his annual stay at the German guest-house, where he could eat the sauerkraut mellowed by the tropical emanations of the local cooking, go to the Easter Saturday dance at La Quebrada and feel "at home" in the dim twilight anonymity of Hornos beach. Of course, we knew that in his younger days he had been a strong swimmer, but what on earth could have induced him at the age of forty, when his health was visibly going from bad to worse, to swim so far out to sea — at midnight, of all things? Frau Müller refused to have a wake at the guest-house, even though he was such a regular guest; instead, that night she organized a dance on the cramped, airless roof-terrace, while Filiberto, ashen-faced in his coffin, waited for the early-morning bus to depart from the bus-station, spending the first night of his new life in the company of packages and crates. When I got there first thing to supervise the loading of the coffin, Filiberto was under a mound of coconuts; the driver told us to hurry up and put him on the roof, covered over with a tarpaulin so as not to upset the passengers, and it had better not be a bad omen for the journey.

We set off from Acapulco, with a breeze still in the air. As we neared Tierra Colorada, the sun began to pound and glare. While eating my breakfast of chorizo and eggs, I opened Filiberto's briefcase, which I had picked up from the Müllers' guest-house the day before, with the rest of his belongings. Two hundred pesos. An old newspaper; some lottery tickets; a one-way travel voucher (why one-way?) and a cheap notebook with its squared pages and marbled cover.

I settled down to read it, notwithstanding the bends, the stench of vomit and a certain natural respect for my dead friend's private life. No doubt it would recall — in effect, that was how it began — our days at the office; perhaps it would explain why he had started falling to pieces, neglecting his responsibilities, dictating garbled letters without reference numbers or due authorization. Why he was finally given the sack, forgoing his pension, despite years of service.

"Today I went to get my pension fixed. The clerk couldn't have been more helpful. It put me in such a good mood that I decided to spend five pesos in a café. The same one that we used to go to in our student days but which nowadays I avoid, since it reminds me how at the age of twenty I could afford more pleasures than I now can at forty. In those days nothing stood between us, any rude remark about any of our friends would have got shouted down; at home, we'd stick up for those whose origins or elegance might be called into question. I knew that many of them — perhaps the poorest — would make it to the top, and that it was here, at college, that the lifelong friendships would be forged that would steer us through life's stormy seas. But it didn't turn out that way. Things didn't obey any pattern. Many of the poor stayed poor; others rose to dizzier heights than any of us could have predicted in those cosy, heated café conversations. While some of us, all set for a promising career, got stuck halfway up the ladder, knocked out of the race by some extra-curricular hurdle, cut off by an invisible chasm from the successes and the failures. Anyway, today I went back to sit on those same chairs — or rather, their updated versions; the soda fountain also seemed to spearhead an invasion — and pretended to go through my files. I saw several of them: changed, oblivious, flourishing, gilded with neon light. Like the café which I barely recognized, like the city itself, they had undergone a remodelling process, leaving me behind. Indeed, they no longer recognized me, or preferred not to recognize me. At most — one or two of them — a brief, flabby pat on the shoulder. *Cheers, how's it going?* Separated from them by the eighteen holes of the Country Club. I masked myself with my files. The years of ambition, of rosy forecasts paraded before me, together with all the minus points that had made them come to nought. I felt the agony of not being able to lay my hands on the past and piece it together like an unfinished jigsaw; but the toy-chest gets left by the wayside and, when it comes to it, there's no way of tracing the lead soldiers, the helmets and wooden swords. All those treasured disguises, for that's all they were. And yet . . . the perseverance, the discipline and dedication had been real enough. Was it insufficient, or was it superfluous? Occasionally I would be assailed by memories of Rilke. The great reward for the adventure of youth has to be death; we must depart while young, taking our secrets with us. Then today there would be no need to look back at the cities of salt. *Five pesos did you say? Take two as a tip.*"

"Apart from his passion for commercial law, Pepe loves theorizing. He spotted me coming out into the central square from the Cathedral, and together we crossed over to the National Palace. He's an agnostic, but he has a hankering for something more: in just half a block's walk, he had to come up with a theory to explain it. Because if he weren't a Mexican, he wouldn't be a Christian and then . . . 'No, look, it's obvious. The Spaniards arrive and they tell you to worship this God who came to a bloody end, wounded in the ribs, nailed to a cross. A sacrificial victim. A propitiatory offering. Faced with notions so close to your own rituals, to your whole way of life, what could be more natural than for you to accept them? Supposing, on the other hand, Mexico had been conquered by Buddhists or Muslims. You can't imagine our indians revering an individual who died of indigestion. But a God who not only has men sacrifice themselves for him, but who goes so far as to have his own heart torn out, that's outdoing Huitzilopochtli at his own game! Christianity — the flesh-and-blood, sacrificial, liturgical side of it — comes to be seen as a novel but logical extension of the native religion. Whereas the parts that have to do with charity, love and the other cheek get discarded. And that sums up Mexico: to believe in someone, you have to kill him.'

"Pepe knew that, since boyhood, I'd kept up an interest in certain forms of native Mexican art. I collect figurines, idols, pots. My weekends are spent at Tlaxcala or Teotihuacán. Maybe that's why he likes to make the theories he elaborates for my benefit relate to such matters. As it happens, for some time now I've been looking for a decent replica of Chac Mool, and today Pepe tells me about a place at La Lagunilla that's got a stone one for sale, at a reasonable price too, it seems. I'll go on Sunday.

"Some joker at work put red ink in the water we keep in a decanter, upsetting everyone's routine. I had to report it to the head of department, who just laughed outright. The culprit took advantage of the fact to make snide remarks behind my back all day long, going on and on about water. Just wait . . ."

"Today, being Sunday, I went to La Lagunilla. I found the statue of Chac Mool in the shop Pepe had mentioned. It's a superb piece of work, life size, and although the dealer assures me it's a genuine original, I've got my doubts. The stone is nothing special, but that doesn't in any way detract from its elegance and solidity. The perfidious salesman has smeared tomato ketchup on its belly to make tourists believe in its gruesome authenticity.

"It cost me more to get it home than to buy it in the first place. But now it's here, for the time being in the cellar while I reorganize the room where I keep my trophies to make space for it. This kind of statue needs brilliant vertical sunlight, as befits its original context and function. It looks wrong in the darkness of the cellar, like some dying creature, reproaching me with a grimace for starving it of light. The shopkeeper had a spotlight on it from above, making its curves three-dimensional, giving my Chac Mool a more friendly expression. I'll have to follow his example."

"I woke up to find the plumbing had gone wrong. Without thinking, I ran the tap in the kitchen sink and it overflowed, pouring on to the floor and running right down to the cellar, before I'd noticed. Chac Mool is no worse for wear as a result of the water, but my suitcases are. It being a weekday, the whole business made me late for the office."

"They've finally been to fix the plumbing. My suitcases are all buckled. And Chac Mool has got green mould round the base."

"I woke up at one in the morning: I'd heard a terrible groaning noise. Thought it might be a burglar. Just imagining things."

"The night-time moans have continued. I can't think what it can be, but it's getting on my nerves. To cap it all, the plumbing went wrong again, and the rain got in, flooding the cellar."

"The plumber still hasn't been, I can't bear it. As for the local authorities, it's useless ringing them. It's the first time the rain has refused to go down the drains and poured into my cellar. The groaning has stopped: if it's not one thing it's another."

"They've drained the cellar, and Chac Mool is covered with mould. It makes him look grotesque, as if the statue's whole surface had broken out in a green rash, except for his eyes which have remained stony. When Sunday comes, I'll scrape off the growth. Pepe has suggested I move to a flat, on the top floor, to avoid such watery disasters. But I can't leave this old house; it may be much too big for one person on his own, and a bit gloomy with its turn-of-the century architecture, but it's the only thing I inherited from my parents and all I have left of them. I couldn't bear to see a soda fountain and jukebox in the cellar, and an interior designer's showroom on the ground floor."

"I went to scrape the mould off Chac Mool with a paint-scraper. It seemed already to have become one with the stone; it took me over an hour, and by the time I'd finished it was six in the evening. I couldn't see clearly in the half-light, and when I finished I ran my hand over the statue's surface. Each time I stroked the stone it seemed to get softer. I couldn't believe it: it was almost like blancmange. That dealer from La Lagunilla has swindled me. His pre-Columbian sculpture is pure plaster, and the damp will ruin it. I've wrapped some towels round it, and tomorrow I'll take it upstairs, before the damage becomes irreparable."

"The towels are on the floor. Extraordinary. I touched Chac Mool again. He's hardened a bit, but he hasn't turned back to stone. I'm reluctant to put it in writing: his torso has something of the texture of skin about it, it yields to the touch like rubber, inside that reclining figure I can feel something flowing . . . I went down again in the evening. There's no doubt about it: Chac Mool has got hairs on his arms."

"This has never happened to me before. I got everything mixed up at the office: I put through a payment that hadn't been authorized, and the undersecretary had to take me to task. I may even have been rude to my colleagues. I'll have to go to the doctor and find out if I'm imagining things or going mad or what, and get rid of that wretched Chac Mool."

Up to this point, Filiberto's handwriting was normal, the same writing I had seen so many times on forms and memos, oval-shaped and well-spaced. The entry for 25 August looked as though it were written by another person. In places the writing was like a child's, with each letter laboriously separate from the others; in other places it was erratic, bordering on the undecipherable. There are three days without an entry, and the story continues:

"It's all so natural; and to think people believe in the real world . . . but this is real, much more so than what I used to believe was real. When you think that a decanter is real, and all the more real, in that we are made more aware of its being, or of its existence, when a joker colours the water red . . . Real the fleeting puff of cigar smoke, real the monstrous image in a circus mirror; and all the dead, past and present, are they not real . . .? If a man were in a dream to walk in Paradise, and were given a flower as proof that he had been there, and if on waking he found that flower in his hand . . . what then? Reality: one day it was shattered into a thousand pieces, the head flew in one direction, the tail in another, and we know only one of the pieces that make up its vast body. The ocean runs free and has no substance; it becomes real only when imprisoned in a shell. Until three days ago, my reality was such that today it has dissolved: nothing but automatic gestures, routine, memory, folders. And then suddenly, just as one day the earth trembles to remind us of its power, or of the death that awaits us, chiding me for my lifelong mindlessness, we come face to face with another reality that we knew was there, waiting to be claimed, and that has to give us a jolt to make us feel its living presence. As before, I thought I was imagining things: Chac Mool, soft and elegant, had changed colour overnight; yellow, almost golden, he seemed to be telling me he was a god, biding his time, more relaxed than before, his smile more benign. And then, yesterday, that catapult out of sleep, with the terrifying certainty that there are two sounds of breathing in the night, that my pulse is not the only one throbbing in the dark. Yes, the sound of footsteps on the stairs. Nightmare. Back to sleep . . . I don't know how long I pretended to be asleep. When I opened my eyes again, it was still not light. The room was filled with a sickening smell, of incense and blood. I ran my unseeing eyes round the bedroom, till they fixed on two flashing orifices, two cutting yellow stripes.

"Not daring to breathe, I switched on the light.

"There was Chac Mool, erect, smiling, ochre-coloured, with his scarlet stomach. I was mesmerized by those two slightly squinting, beady eyes, set close to his triangular nose. His lower teeth were sunk, rigid, into his upper lip; only the glint of the square skullcap on that unwieldy head betrayed any sign of life. Chac Mool advanced towards the bed; at that moment it started to rain."

I remember that, at the end of August, Filiberto was dismissed from the office, with an official reprimand from the head of department, amid rumours of madness and even embezzlement of funds. That I couldn't believe. But I did see some crazy letters, asking the chief clerk if water had a smell, offering his services to the Chairman of the Water Board to make it rain in the desert. I didn't know what to make of it; I thought that the rain, exceptionally heavy that summer, was getting to him. Or that he was suffering from depression as a result of living in that rambling old house, with half the rooms locked and covered in dust, with no servants or relatives to look after him. The following jottings correspond to the end of September:

"Chac Mool can be nice when he feels like it . . . the babbling of an enraptured brook . . . He knows fantastic stories about the monsoons, the tropical rains, the scourge of the desert; every plant descends from his mythical parentage: the willow, his wayward daughter; the lotus, his favourite; his mother-in-law: the cactus. What I can't stand is the smell, unlike anything human, of that flesh that is not flesh, of those sandals irradiating antiquity. Cackling with laughter, Chac Mool describes how he was discovered by Le Plongeon, and put in touch, physically speaking, with men who believed in other symbols. His spirit has lived, as a force of nature, in the water-pitcher and the rainstorm; his stone is another matter, and to have prised it out of its hiding-place is both unnatural and unkind. I think that's something Chac Mool will never forgive. He knows all about the imminence of the aesthetic act.

"I had to give him some kitchen cleaner to wash off the ketchup the dealer smeared on his belly thinking he was Aztec. He didn't seem to like my asking about his relationship to Tláloc and, when he gets angry, his teeth, which are repulsive at the best of times, glint and grind. The first few days, he went downstairs to sleep in the cellar; as from yesterday in my bed."

"The dry season has started. Yesterday, from the drawing-room where I now sleep, I started to hear the same moans and groans as at the beginning, followed by terrible crashing sounds. I went upstairs and half-opened the bedroom door: Chac Mool was smashing the lamps, the furniture; he leapt at the door with his lacerated hands, and I barely had time to slam it shut and hide in the bathroom . . . Later he came downstairs panting and asked for some water; he keeps the taps running all day long, there's not an inch of the house left dry. I have to wrap up tight at night, and I've asked him to stop the water in the drawing-room."*

"Today Chac Mool flooded the drawing-room. In exasperation I told him I was going to take him back to La Lagunilla. Only his snigger — chillingly different from any laughter of man or beast — could have instilled as much fear in me as the blow he gave me with his arm weighed down with heavy bracelets. I've got to face up to it: I'm his prisoner. My original intention had been different: I would control Chac Mool as one controls a toy; perhaps it was a relic of my childhood arrogance; but childhood — as someone once said — is a fruit devoured by the years, had I but realized . . . He's taken to borrowing my clothes, and he puts on a dressing-gown when he starts to sprout green fungus. Chac Mool is used to being obeyed at all times; having never had to give orders, I can only submit. As long as it doesn't rain — so much for his magic powers — his moods and tantrums will continue."

"Today I discovered that Chac Mool goes out of the house at night. At dusk, he always sings an old, tuneless song, older than song itself. Then it stops. I knocked at his door several times, and as there was no reply I plucked up courage to go in. The

* Filiberto doesn't explain in what language he communicated with Chac Mool.

bedroom, which I hadn't been into since the day the statue tried to attack me, is a shambles, and it's here that the stench of incense and blood that has permeated the house is at its strongest. But, behind the door, there are bones: bones of dogs, of mice and cats. That's what Chac Mool steals in the night to feed himself on. That explains the terrible barking early in the morning."

"February. Dry. Chac Mool watches my every step; he's made me phone a restaurant to order chicken risotto to be delivered every day. But the money appropriated from work is about to run out. The inevitable happened; as from the first of the month, they've cut off the water and electricity because of the unpaid bills. But Chac has discovered a public drinking-fountain a couple of blocks away; every day I make ten or a dozen excursions to fetch water, and he surveys me from the roof. He says that, if I try to make a run for it, he'll strike me down; he's the God of Lightning too. What he doesn't know is that I know about his nightly escapades . . . As there's no electricity, I have to go to bed at eight. I ought to be used to Chac Mool by now, but the other day I bumped into him on the stairs in the dark, I felt his clammy arms, his scaly refurbished skin, and almost screamed out loud.

"If it doesn't rain soon, Chac Mool will turn back to stone. I've noticed that of late he's been having difficulty walking; sometimes he stays in a reclining position for hours on end, in a state of paralysis, looking like an idol again. But such moments of relaxation only give him renewed energy to assault and claw me, as if he could draw liquid from my flesh. The friendly interludes when he used to tell me ancient tales have stopped; I can sense the resentment building up inside him. Other signs have set me thinking; he keeps fondling the silk of my dressing-gowns; he wants me to bring a maid to the house; he's made me teach him to use soap and after-shave. I think Chac Mool is succumbing to human temptations; there are even signs of ageing in that face that seemed ageless. That could be my salvation: if Chac becomes human, maybe all those centuries of life will suddenly converge, crushing him under their weight. But that could equally be the source of my downfall: Chac won't want me to witness his demise, he may decide to kill me.

"Today I'm going to take advantage of Chac's midnight outing to run away. I'll go to Acapulco; we'll see what can be done in the way of finding work, to tide me over till Chac Mool dies: there's no doubt that the time is drawing near; his hair is greying, his joints are swollen. I need to take the sun, swim, recover my strength. I've got four hundred pesos left. I'll go to the Müllers' guest-house, it's cheap and comfortable. Chac Mool can have the house to himself: I wonder how long he'll last without my buckets of water."

Filiberto's diary ends at this point. I didn't want to dwell on his story; I slept all the way to Cuernavaca. From there to Mexico City I tried to make some sense of his text, by explaining it in terms of overwork or some psychological motive. When we pulled in at the bus-station at nine o'clock at night, I still had not been able to figure out the nature of my friend's madness. I hired a van to take the coffin to Filiberto's house, in order to make the funeral arrangements from there.

Before I could insert the key into the lock, the door opened. A yellow-skinned indian appeared, in a dressing-gown, with a scarf round his neck. His appearance could not have been more repulsive; he reeked of cheap after-shave; his face was plastered with powder, trying to camouflage the wrinkles; his lips were daubed with lipstick, and his hair looked as though it were dyed.

"I beg your pardon . . . I didn't know Filiberto had . . ."

"That's quite all right; I know all about it. Tell the men to take the body down to the cellar."

Translated by Jo Labanyi

Number One Son

Pedro Shimose

*B*ack in the days when Ali Baba was boiling the forty thieves in oil, our dear general made a parachute jump to prove what a man he was, and Doña Candelaria had to go back to her hut with a bundle of dirty washing. At that very moment I was eating my piece of cake with slices of bitter orange. Shit! What a toothache! "That's what you get for eating all that rubbish," Engracia said as she walked past, wiggling her hips. They're mine, they're yours, come and get it on all fours, they whispered, so off I went with her. Got a toothache? Come on, I'll take care of it for you. OK so perhaps I shouldn't have gone off like that with a hot piece of stuff who peroxides her hair, but what the hell, I'm a big boy now, I've done my military service so no one's going to tell me how to behave. Anyway, Engracia is a good, loving woman.

Rosendo Peinado woke up early and brushed his teeth with quinine powder. May Day. Happy birthday, boss! Some joke: his birthday on the day of the workers! Salina's band roused him with a fanfare. Then Happy Birthday to me! His bodyguards fired off their guns in salute. Hey there, get them all a drink will you, a beer or whatever they fancy. Go on, get stuck into it. But Choco, make sure your men keep their eyes peeled, we wouldn't want Kimura's son to come and spoil the party, would we?

Rosendo felt something uncomfortable on the back of his neck. Something cold and hard. He opened his eyes and saw a smiling Kuni Kimura sitting next to him, pressing a long-barrelled Colt .38 against his neck. He was so scared he sobered up at once. "Happy birthday Don Rosendo, I've come to kill you." Only a few hours before Don Rosendo had warned him:

"Listen to me, you asshole chink. You've got twenty-four hours to get out of town. If you don't . . ." Rosendo, the honourable Don Rosendo Peinado, Doctor Peinado, the boss of the town, gestured as if to say: "We'll lay you out right here."

Kuni remembered how his father had died. Back in '45, at the start of nineteenhundredandfortyfive. Rosendo Peinado and his thugs had surrounded Kimurasan's house. Tied him up. Bound him hand and foot. "The Allies are rounding up all the filthy skunks who are against our democracies."

"I not do . . ."

"You're a stinkin' fifth columnist."

"Not be so."

"You're a Japanese spy."

"Kimurasan: we need twenty bottles of alcohol for all the boys here. Come on, get those cases of Zeller Moller out." Rosendo Peinado, candidate for the Revolutionary Socialist Party, was inflamed again with hate as he recalled those days prior to the election. Kimurasan had refused to give him any alcohol to get the locals drunk with. "That's what those chink bastards are like, they've no gratitude to this country. They come here to Bolivia, make their fortune, and then turn round and refuse to help the government. I'll teach them a lesson they won't forget." The bottles of alcohol up on the cart. Death to the opposition! Some figures flit by with lighted torches. The sun bursts on a night sky. Then the dark engulfs the madness.

Doña Lastenia told me how they finished off my father. They took him out into the countryside with two Germans. They shouted insults at them, beat and kicked them, made them dig their own graves. The yankee priests refused them the last rites. They said they were heathens condemned to hell anyway. When the holes were ready . . . ratatat . . . bursts of automatic fire, so long, it's been good to know you. Bolivia the one and only!

Rosendo Peinado quit politics to devote himself to business. With my father's money, with the lands and plantations of other Japanese, Italian and German settlers. Everyone knows that.

War is hard on some, but good to others. Others like Rosendo Peinado. You should have seen him riding my father's favourite roan. You never know who you're working for in the end . . . there's nothing you can do, except look after number one.

He cut the motor and jumped onto dry land. For the first time his tooth began to ache again. The noise of the engine chugchugging upstream, the gleam of his cigarettes as he puffed on them. The kid in the t-shirt didn't have much to say. He hadn't opened his mouth in the whole journey. All he did was shuffle a pack of cards and oil his long Colt .38. He counted the bullets, from time to time tested his aim by firing at animals on the river banks, bits of floating timber, water birds. The bullet follows my eye, and what follows the bullet?

The president had said: "Aha, what about our tradition of political asylum? What about sacred freedom of choice, respect for the dignity of man? America for the world. America for freedom. And so on and so forth . . ." Then the ever-present eunuchs went and whispered to the gringos: "How would you like the little runts, wrapped or as they come?" To which the gringos replied, "Just as they come, that'll do nicely." That's how the pages of history are written, and that's how fortunes are made in these countries of ours blessed by a gracious God. So they took over everything, and were honourable, respectable citizens. Peinado's cronies wasted all their money on orgies and women. But Rosendo Peinado knew how to make the best of his windfall. He was seen at all the smart occasions. He hobnobbed with the aristocrats, did dirty work for the oligarchs. Took part in laying foundation stones and attended Revolutionary Socialist political meetings. Don Rosendo's fortune grew and grew. People forgot the past and everywhere they swore that Don Rosendo had been born a rich man. "He was always rich and honest." When the Revolutionary Socialists collapsed, Don Rosendo signed up with the opposition. When the cookie crumbles, don't stick around to pick up the pieces . . . happiness is a full belly . . . a bird in the stomach is worth a hundred flying around . . . up with the opposition!

The youngster in a t-shirt was pointing a revolver at him. He motioned for him to stand up. Rosendo Peinado looked outside and saw all his bodyguards swinging in mid-air. It was then he realized Engracia had betrayed him. They're mine, they're yours, come and get it on all fours . . . "A drug," Kumi patiently explained. A moon on the wane and his gang all dangling at the end of a rope. The chill of dawn. The church clock struck five. Don Rosendo threw up. Carts were lumbering to market as the cocks drove off the last shadows of night.

They had all come out to greet him with their posters: WE WANT ELEKTRIC   LONG LIVE DOCTOR PEYNADO   WE NEED A SKOOL. A loudspeaker playing an Andean tune. The day for announcing the candidates was dawning. "There's a southerly brewing," an old woman said. Candidates were adopted two years ahead of time just in case. Those yellow glittering eyes. The skeletal bodies tanned by years of sun. Those empty, bony hands. Ears tired of always hearing the same promises. Up on the bandstand in the main square, Rosendo Peinado spouts and spouts.

His party came nowhere. But that didn't stop the doctor. Doctor Peinado made a little trip to Switzerland. Claimed it was for health reasons. The opposition accused him of keeping a fat account in a Swiss bank. Everyone said it, no one could prove it. When he got back, Doctor Peinado found that the price of rubber had gone through the floor, and chestnuts weren't so hot either. The only thing going up was the cost of living. The rich countries got richer and the poor got poorer. Peinado travelled to the capital, made contacts, held meetings with people who could pull strings. Evil tongues claimed Peinado had become a freemason even though he was great friends with the bishop and, thanks to the usual political intrigues, also enjoyed the support of the top brass in the military junta. Three cheers for our good doctor!

Now Peinado is digging his own grave. The number one son is keeping watch. Blisters on his hands. Blisters that hurt and bleed. Sweat. Birds in the trees, flowers, the smell of the jungle, sweet-scented trees, ants, snakes ... Peinado thought of his wife and children, his three legitimate children. He didn't spare a thought for all the others. How he regretted having abandoned that good woman, who had stood by him through all the hard times when he, Rosendo Peinado, had been nothing more than a poor wretch without a hole to crawl into. "Dig faster, asshole." A well-aimed kick sent him writhing in pain. He groaned moaned groaned as he dug the grave.

The Oasis bar and brothel, where temptation falls into everyone's lap. Schoolkids went there to make men of themselves, to experience life and get laid with bountiful Brazilian and Peruvian whores. No dirty indians in here if you please. Whaddayamean why? All right, but even if they could get in, what would they do then, just a drink would cost them an arm and a leg. What about the students then? They all had fathers to look after them. Living out of their pockets. No common soldiers either. The conscripts were freighted out to pick chestnuts. The officers did good business hiring them out. So many soldiers for so many hours, equals so much. Dough for the general, and the doughboys eat pigswill. That's the way this cookie life crumbles, I'm in charge so be ready to jump ... Kuni stood leaning against the wall in a corner, shuffling his pack of cards. Doctor Peinado came in with his gang of thugs. "Play 'Palm Trees' for me!" he shouted, while his sidekick ordered drinks all round.

> Tell me that it's true
> the dream I had last night
> that it's only me
> your arms are holding tight

One person refused to drink. Peinado told the musicians to stop playing. He heard the voice of a youngster in a black t-shirt. "Watch out Don Rosendo, I'm going to kill you." Then he left. Rosendo's guards wanted to go after him, but he stopped them. "Let him go." The celebrations continued. Roll out the barrel, roll out the fun. When Rosendo Peinado was good and drunk he sent his men to fetch Kuni Kimura. They were back with him in a few minutes. They'd had their fun roughing him up. They pushed him against the wall. "Listen kid, stop messing with me, or I'll lose my patience and get one of my friends here to deal with you." He pointed to his men. "I'll give you twenty-four hours to get out of town."

The grave was finished. More than anything, Peinado wished he was somewhere else, on some other planet. He heard the sound of a gun being cocked.

Rosendo Peinado stood up, startled and bathed in sweat. He had fallen asleep in his hammock. So it had all been a bad dream. He cursed. Cockroaches are immortal. He started to look around him, when behind his back he heard the sound of a long Colt .38 being cocked.

Translated by Nick Caistor

Princess Caucubú Goes Shopping

Roberto Urias

TEACHER: "Who was Christopher Columbus?"
PUPIL: "A nasty German who was so crazy for
pepper he killed all the indians and brought the
black slaves, who refused to work."

*P*erhaps calling her a princess is an exaggeration. In fact,
Caucubú is only the daughter of the chieftain Manatigua-
huraguana, better known as Tabo, lord and master of the fields
and village of Mancanilla, today's Santiago de Cuba. But since in
these proletarian, tropical lands of ours there's no shortage of
chiefs, maybe the title is appropriate. And it could be due to her
ancestry that Caucubú is known as "the prettiest little indian in
all Guamuhaya." Like the skilful wordsmiths we are, legends
about her abound, passed from mouth to mouth to a backdrop
of flames of guayaba logs, the glitter of vineleaves and thrones of
palm fronds decked in lilies. In other words, a real ritzy soap
opera.

Yet, leaving aside all the enchantment of legend, the real story
of Princess Caucubú, who is over five hundred years old now, is,
as they say here in Cuba, "well worth a look". Or rather, it's a
story that's both sweet and harsh, like the taste of pineapples
which grow and thrive in our country, and are exported, along
with big mommas of tomatoes, by Cubafrutas Inc.

Many, many moons have licked the reeds of our rivers since
the arrival of the Spaniards disrupted the rhythm of Taino
indian life, which wasn't worth writing home about anyway,
what with all those mosquitoes and the lack of electricity. To tell
the truth, Princess Caucubú wasn't as taken with the indian
Narido as the eternal romantics claim, because she was dazzled
by the physical charms and Made in Spain clothes of some of the
white men. So she finished up as the adoring and adored lover of
one Ojeda (blond and blue-eyed, of course), who, for business
reasons (conquest and colonization, disguised behind the

Roberto Urias

motto "Christianity or Death"), took her with him on the back of a splendid chestnut mare to far-flung regions such as Sabaneque, Jagua, Camagüey and Guacanayabo. Caucubú always loved to travel, and so ... lulled by endless greenery, the call of the mocking-birds and the boom of the Spaniards' firearms, the happy couple celebrated their babylonic nuptials, without the Caribbean so much as blushing.

For several centuries they learned to live together with no great dramas, without bitterness or traumas that might have called for psychiatrists or pharmacists, for richer, for poorer, until Princess Caucubú has become this woman of today, Juanita Rodríguez, "the indian", daughter of Tota and Tabo, living and loving in a tenement on Teniente Rey Street in old Havana, who boasts as proof of her lofty ancestry and Cubanity not only a plaster statue of the Virgin of Charity from El Cobre on her altar at home, and a gold medal of her between her breasts, but also the changes time has etched into her features: straight black hair, green eyes, thick lips and fiery thighs like the mulattas at the Tropicana nightclub. Juanita is, to put it in our best Cuban manner, a rich and spicy dish ideally suited to these hot climes of ours ...

And, like every other Tabo, Ricardo and Juanita, our revolutionized princess has set off today to do her shopping since, in accordance with the rationing established for industrial goods (yes, you heard me right, and may future generations forgive us), today is the day for her group, letter and number. Today and no other. Nothing for it then but to get her card stamped at work, then to rush to see what they've "drawn" in the stores. Really, "drawn" as in a lottery is the only way to convey the delirium, the "shot of adrenalin" feeling we all enjoy, when we go off to claim our "prize".

After spending most of the morning in a vain search for the thousand and one things she needed: shampoo, deodorant, a pair of panties that fitted, beginning to feel overwhelmed yet again by the unequal struggle that is daily life in this our vale of tears (water-sprinklers, bolero and all the rest) princess Juanita

Rodríguez decided to end her *via crucis* along Galliano Street and go home. Then, praise be! she saw a long, tempting line outside La Victoria store, and leapt to join it. She soon learnt that this time they'd "drawn" some portable Siboney radios. Her lifelong Taino dream!

She wasn't too put off by the card in the window warning there were "no batteries". Once she'd bought the radio she would find some way to adapt it, maybe even that old Kato crane generator would come in handy. She was so carried away she herself could have provided the electricity for her Siboney; she could see it now installed in her beach hut, plastic turning to tortoiseshell as they grew old together.

So our princess fell in behind Luz Divina, a coal black Cuban momma, three layers of make-up and a family-sized swaying backside. After her came Concha Ruíz, from Galicia in Spain no less, as white as milk and fat as a beached whale. Next in line was Widow Wong, wearing pebble glasses and her plait as long as the queue they were in. Last but not least, Ernesto, alias Sweet Pickle, said by malicious tongues to be as queer as they come. Nothing for it but to wait and wait, praying they would achieve their portable, musical dream. Waiting in the clammy bosom of this August day, rapidly reducing them all to "iguanaism", the kind of beatific stupor that comes from standing out so long in the sun, mouth open and drooling like so many decrepit old iguanas. And Juanita, who has never read Mr Joyce, but who has lived a full life, drifts into a playpainful monologue:

"It's hot a lot in Cuba! If only I had a nice ice. Cuban ice is nice but cola ice keeps you cooler. Cool fools in the queue on cue for ice cubes. The country of cubes discovered by cool Columbus with his collection of coolies and lumberjacks, all for its nice ices, so the earth is a cool cube? Cue who? Who'll queue and cry Cuba a cube my kingdom for a cube? A can of cola with a cube of ice keeps you cooler in the queue shiver from collar to colon so long Columbus can you decide as side by side we stand in line waiting to collect the correct connection our cool collective corrective collapse, collapse . . ."

Princess Caucubú, alias Juanita Rodríguez "the indian", was lost in these metaphysical considerations when she heard the daily war cry "They're pushing in." Sweet Pickle had spotted two black friends of Luz Divina in the line.

"Keep your cool, boy, we only came for a chat," one of the newcomers said, fanning herself with a piece of cardboard. "Mind you, if our friend Divi here could get her hands on a nice little radio for each of us, we wouldn't complain," the other one added.

"You don't say! Over my dead body," thundered Concha Ruíz, and Juanita realized there was going to be trouble. She thought: "The gang's all here, let the show begin."

"Hey, what's got into Moby Dick?" Luz Divina shouted.

"A little more respect, lady; I never called you a black slave, did I?" Carmen sobbed, red in the face. Her words had no effect on the Kikuyu sisters:

"Black slave your grandma, cheeseball."

Juanita kept her silence as the missiles flew and the conflagration escalated.

"The only cheese around here is between your legs, loud-mouth," the Galician warrior struck back.

"My God, you can't imagine how much I need that radio," Widow Wong lamented.

"Yea, of course, if not four eyes here will die of homesickness," Divina stabbed.

To which Wong replied in her best inscrutable manner: "Don't put me down like that, I have my needs too."

"Needs, tell me about them. I have to get a radio so I can swap it for a pot of skin cream for my brother," sighed Sweet Pickle the martyr.

"Shut it, you old hen, it was the likes of you brought chaos upon us," one of the black women spat.

"This country is the original chaos," Widow Wong decreed.

Everything descended into melodrama when Concha Ruíz suddenly broke down and cried: "I'm a sick woman, and my husband's away fighting in Angola."

"Poor thing, so what she's suffering from is a lack of vitamin P. Why doesn't he send you some from Africa?" asked Luz Divina with her snake's tongue.

Then Sweet Pickle, bathed in sweat and swaying to and fro with an enormous green bag on his shoulder, declared: "Columbus is to blame for everything."

"Whaddayoumean, it's that Simón Bolívar who messed everything up, thinking he was Napoleon and causing all that independence nonsense," Concha Ruíz replied.

"That's what you reckon, is it? And what about that sonofabitch padre Las Casas?" Luz Divina wanted to know.

"No, it's Saint Hippolyte who's to blame for all our troubles," Widow Wong whispered. Everyone's eyes opened wide, trying to understand what she meant . . .

Mass hysteria had taken such a hold that Princess Caucubú, who until then had been watching with amusement, decided she should restore some order. With aristocratic gestures and best "Radio Encyclopedia" voice, she started to put them straight once and for all:

"What is all this? How long are you going to carry on with all this bullshit? It's too hot to be swapping insults and fighting about the colour of your skin: 'black slave', 'cheeseball', 'rinkydink chink'. It's not the moment to be washing our linen in public like this, or trying to find someone to blame for our troubles. The worlds you all came from — tearing each other's hair, shouting — they're all long gone, they flew about as far as the balloonist Matías Perez, i.e. a few feet and straight to the bottom. What matters is the world we're in now, and where we're headed. And since we're all on this raft together, what matters most is to avoid anyone rocking the boat and sending us all down below. You've got to keep your cool: aspirin or camomile tea before you start to fight. And keep the faith: Our Lady is powerful and will never abandon us. We're all the same in her eyes, and what we need is to keep our wits about us, so the bigshots here and elsewhere aren't always telling us what to do . . ."

Juanita was really warming to her sermon when a voice — one of those off-mike that can sometimes puncture all the dramatic tension — suddenly announced: "No more Siboneys, none for anyone." This produced an explosion of shouts, an epic tumult, a flood of idiosyncrasy, an effusion of popular lyricism, as some official folklore expert might put it in his bureaucratic report.

"Assholes," Luz Divina summed it up.

"I'm off to the clinic to have my pressure checked," Concha Ruíz announced, well and truly harpooned.

"I'm glad they've run out, those radios are shit useless anyway," Widow Wong pronounced, pulling out a peanut bar.

"Just my stinkin' luck. I'll be putting aloes on my skin till it turns to leather," Sweet Pickle moaned.

By now they all looked like steaming coffee pots under the August Havana sun. Only Princess Caucubú, alias Juanita Rodríguez, "the indian", was still cool and relaxed, as if the hurricane that had swept over them had passed her by. She simply said: "I'm off, I've dried peas to soak." And off she went, humming to herself the words of a song to the Virgin; "stick, stick, stand by me and do the trick . . ."

Translated by Nick Caistor

The Peace of the Dead

Ana Valdés

*T*he room smelt strangely of formaldehyde. He remembered the smell from his father's laboratory, from his own experiences dissecting small animals. Rats, unwanted cats, pigeons. He used to copy his father's movements, the precise slit with the knife, a rapid injection, agile hands suturing, stitching. His mother always used to say his father was in the wrong profession, that with those clever hands of his he should have been a tailor, someone who sewed uniforms and wedding dresses.

My father would laugh at this and threaten to take her at her word. He'd set up shop in the Jewish quarter of the city, where nearly all the other tailors and seamstresses were crowded. "And the smell of leather and chalk, long curly beards and halva . . ."

I wanted to be a doctor like him, but I didn't have the talent, his ability to diagnose an illness almost as soon as he saw a slightly enlarged pupil or a wincing smile that disguised pain. So I had to make do studying subjects related to medicine that left me nervous and frustrated, with the bittersweet taste of defeat always weighing me down.

Which explains this freshly whitewashed room, my first office, crammed with books and files. Strange that it should be here in this museum, the most famous in the city, where my father and I used to spend our happiest Sundays together, peering at bows and arrows, shields, ritual masks, ceremonial pillars.

The museum prides itself on being unique in the world for such a huge collection of objects culled from the widest range of human groups and periods of history: more than two thousand disappeared nations. Assyrian lions caught by the sculptor at the moment of leaping; Babylonian parchments that tell of the immortal hero Gilgamesh; carved bone harpoons from Nova Scotia and Greenland. "The generations of man are like leaves, they fall and others take their place."

And so on through the nations, tribes, kingdoms and empires that have followed one after another on this earth. Vain attempts to hold up the passage of time, to imprison it in boxes containing far worse misfortunes than those Pandora saved up. Now they are no more than a few lines in an encyclopedia, a fragment of knowledge lodged in the mind of some wise old man.

I often think of this bitter destiny that awaits all those of us who are flesh and blood; I sometimes dream of those ancestors who picked lemons and oranges, had children, watched them grow and then die. I learnt about them in sterile classes larded with lifeless statistics, but nobody was ever able to tell me what those men who died so long ago had felt or dreamt.

Helsingor, Montenegro, Pergamo, dust to dust. Charrúas, Maoris, Mayas, Dakotas, Blackfeet, Hurons, Mohicans, Minoas and Guenoas, Patagonians, Lapps, Olmecs: nothing but remains and relics, pillaged tombs, excavations, palaces covered with sand and seaweed, jungle which suddenly parts and a bewildered peasant sees something glinting, a terracotta profile that reminds him of his own face.

The other face stares at him from beneath a helmet decked with blue feathers stretching down to the waist, rings of gold and precious stone hanging from a mutilated ear. A prince from beyond time, he looks pityingly on this wretched descendant of his. Vanity of vanities, the remains of his race are condemned to exhibition in museum showcases, to adorn the triumphal procession of an archaeologist through great cities.

The peasant chops a hole in the greenery and Palenque stands before him in all its majesty, the priests' palace, the pyramid-grave and its golden sarcophagus, houses stacked with offerings, places of rest and prayer for believers who have flocked from far.

I have accompanied several professors on expeditions like this; I too have cut my way through leaves and trees undisturbed since the beginning of time. Sometimes I have felt I was a desecrator, lifting veils it was better not to lift, profaning treasures and remains that the ages have clothed in their dust.

But most of my time is spent classifying other people's discoveries, the plunder that reaches the museum in the form of ragged bits of clothing, clumsy tools, weapons filched from some battlefield that may have been the Verdun of its day.

The smell is odd. This is not a natural science museum, we don't keep anything here that is or has ever been alive.

Professor Leclerc left his office and walked down corridors he had never before explored. He followed his sense of smell, a bloodhound lost in a maze. The smell seemed to come from a large room, where men in blue overalls wearing oxygen masks were coming and going. Curious, he asked what was going on, and was told that they were cleaning and injecting the mummies and skeletons in the museum's collection, something that was done every five years to keep off insects and maggots.

He was given protective clothing, and went into the room. What he saw reminded him of the catacombs, or the charnel house of the Square des Innocents, where the bones of Parisians had been piled from the city's foundation until the seventeenth century.

Yet this was a museum. What was the purpose of all these countless mummies and bodies in various states of conservation, skeletons sometimes complete, more often no more than a tibia or a skull, a smashed pelvis?

In dusty reports he read about the Hallness-MacGregory Arctic Expedition which had left New York with the apparent intention of gathering rare specimens of the fauna and flora of the Arctic: "blue-tinged spiders which reproduced calmly in the midst of iceflows and glaciers; pale, delicately hued flowers." But the real reason for the expedition had been to collect well-preserved mummies and skeletons which could throw new light on the origins of man in the New World and his relation with other human groups. Had he crossed the Bering Straits when they were solid ice, had he sailed across the Pacific on rafts?

Interest had been awakened in this far-flung region when in 1885 an old hunter had sold the museum six mummies he claimed to have found on the Faar Islands, close to the Arctic Circle. Thanks to his instructions it had been relatively easy to discover the spot. It was a small island almost entirely covered with primitive crypts and caves dug in the rocks. The masterpiece of this rough mausoleum was a crypt concealed beneath skilfully carved wooden boards and cured sealskins. When the crypt was opened, the explorers found bird feathers carefully sewn together, ivory needles and harpoons, stone lamps and containers full of amber. There were also four shrouds, which were found to contain the well-preserved bodies of two men, a woman and a young girl.

As he read more reports, Professor Leclerc felt increasingly uneasy. What scientific reasons could have justified such profanities? He recalled his studies in law when they were told of the legal penalties for defilers of crypts. Not even Madame de Montespan had escaped severe punishment after being found guilty of celebrating black masses and stealing corpses. She and Lavoisin confessed to having robbed graves and holding secret ceremonies in the Lachaise cemetery. The same Père Lachaise cemetery where today the most ancient part is closed, abandoned to cats with spectral eyes and gleaming fur.

That night he had his first nightmares. The dead from every age crowded round him, demanding to be allowed to rest. His dreams were filled with fleshless hands and eyes empty in their sockets, mouths with no tongues imploring him to open the museum and set them free.

He woke up in a foul temper which his little morning rituals — a shower, shaving the blue bristles of his beard which grew overnight like a second skin — did nothing to dispel. Not even a breakfast of strong coffee and orange juice could lift his spirits. He spent the morning walking, in the hope that this would clear his head. Until he felt better, he wouldn't set foot in the museum. He wandered into a local cinema, where a sleepy projectionist was showing a Western to an audience of half a dozen teenagers. He had to leave when the red indians came on the screen. They looked just like the dead in his nightmares, with their leathery faces. Behind the images he could see the macabre grins of the mummies fixed for ever in time.

This went on for several days. At night he drank to fend off his dreams, in the morning he was restless, anxious. He finally decided to talk to his father, who always could be trusted to come up with an answer.

His parents had not wanted him to move out; the family home was too big for them without him. Once they had realized that their arguments were useless, they offered to buy him a small apartment near the museum. They doted on this intelligent, stubborn only child of theirs. They could deny him nothing. François had been such a model child that at times they worried about him. When other children were breaking windows with footballs, he was reading or dissecting animals in his father's laboratory; while the other boys were testing their wings with their school companions, he was meditating in the mountains. They were still not quite sure whether he was a mystic or a daydreamer.

He entered the house without ringing: his parents had insisted he keep the key. His bedroom could have gone on display in the museum: on the desk were the books which had shaped him as an adolescent, Pavese, Sartre, Pratolini, Salinger. Those were his existentialist years, when he always wore black and listened to Juliette Greco and Bob Dylan. He found his parents in the living-room. His father was reading and smoking a pipe, his mother as ever knitting for the poor: yardlong scarves, shapeless jerseys, woollen shawls for winter.

"Is that you, François? What a nice surprise. We thought you had far too much work to come and visit your poor old distant relations."

His father's clinical eye was bound to spot the symptoms of

insomnia, alcohol and nightmares at once. The best thing was to tell him everything straight out. But first the three of them had dinner. His mother was a wonderful cook, capable of performing alchemy in the copper pans she had inherited from her grandmother. He and his father often joked with her, saying that Paracelsus and Zeno had been wrong to search for the Philosopher's Stone in all those old Egyptian and Hebrew manuscripts, when all the time she had the secret in her cooking pots, which were capable of transforming thyme and basil or of sublimating meat and flour. His parents thought he looked thinner, pestered him with questions about his work, his plans. They had been thrilled to read an announcement in the paper about his appointment as emeritus professor and his academic successes.

After dinner, he abruptly asked: "Did you know there are more than 400,000 skeletons and mummies of aboriginal and primitive peoples in our museums?"

His father looked at him in surprise. "I didn't realize there were so many. I knew there must be lots, although they are not on open display to avoid any ethical or moral problems. I remember the Musée de l'Homme once did an exhibition of a small indigenous group that's extinct today, the Charrúas I think they were called."

François was astonished yet again at his father's encyclopedic memory, for which no piece of information was useless. Despite his years, nothing was lost to his agile, trained mind.

The two of them consulted books, looked up dates. They were amazed at the figures. Well-informed sources calculated that in the attics of the Smithsonian Institution alone there were more than 18,500 human specimens. Not to mention the Natural History Museum in New York, the Museum of Anthropology in Mexico City, the Dahlem in Berlin, the Vatican. François also learned that it was not only the most remote tribes and people who had been robbed of their relics and their bones: he read of an archaeological dig in the north of Sweden, near Ornskoldvik, which had found an Iron Age village with excellently preserved skeletons. The archaeologists had hailed the discovery as one of the most important of modern times, and had taken the bones for tests with carbon 14 and infra-red rays. But the Swedish church had protested: these people were from the time of bishop Ansgar, who, with his disciple Olmar, had been sent to the Scandinavian peninsula by the emperor Louis the Pious to bring the faith to Ostrogoths, Visigoths, Germans and Finns. Their remains should be left in consecrated ground, or were they somehow less worthy believers than the people of today? What would happen on Judgment Day, when the archangels' trumpets open all the tombs, and the bones of the dead are reborn as bodies in glory? Were the scientists willing to take responsibility for all those lost souls searching for their mortal remains in museums and laboratories round the world? The theological debates raged on; the archaeologists were threatened by fundamentalist groups.

François went home feeling relieved. His scientific mind had needed facts and figures for him to be able to act.

The next day his office seemed gloomier than ever, with a week's post waiting to be answered. The smell of formaldehyde had gone, but he knew that the mummies were still there, in the big room, waiting for the end of time. The different ways and images by which mankind had imagined that moment flashed through his mind: the four horsemen of the apocalypse, Ragnarok, the Titans freed from their chains. Did all the dead, from so many different places and times, believe in some kind of resurrection, in Anubis imagining human lives as light as feathers?

The mummies of the Charrúa people stared at him from their glass cases. They had been exhibited as the last remnants of a fierce, warlike people who had made the colonization of the Rio de la Plata costly in lives. It was also true that the region had few minerals and was classified for many years by the Spaniards as "land of no useful value", until the cattle and horses which had roamed wild and multiplied turned the area into the American continent's greatest producer of salted and jerked beef. This brought prosperity, fenced-off fields, the railway, meatpackers, chilled meat plants. There was no room for the Charrúas in this brave new world. They had to be got rid of; they were only a minor tribe, unremarkable hunters and potters. They were in no way comparable to their Inca or Aztec neighbours, who had been almost as civilized as Europeans. As in the Aztec city of Tenochtitlán, which had led Bernal Díaz to exclaim: "Not even in Venice have I seen such well-built palaces."

There were five of them, four men and one woman. Senaque, Peru, Tacuabé, Guyunusa, baptised Micaëla by the Christians, and lastly Ramón Matajo. A Frenchman had bought them cheaply as prisoners of war, dragged along behind the remains of Bernabé Rivera, killed at the battle of Yacaré Cururú. The sea journey to France must have seemed like one long nightmare to them, accustomed only to travelling in rough and ready canoes on the swift rivers of their lands. "Water rushing ever onwards, willows and guava trees, river of birds."

They had arrived in winter, one of those grey, windy Parisian winters. The Eiffel Tower was a new and already redundant shape on the skyline in a city that Haussmann had redrawn. Wide boulevards for carriages and cannon to speed along. The 1871 barricades were still fresh in the memory of the politicians, who knew that the people of Paris could not be taken lightly. That ferocious people of the St Bartholomew Night massacre, who cheered on Coligny's murderer; that people who, led by washerwomen and artisans, had ransacked the Faubourg Saint Antoine and torn down the walls of the Bastille with their bare hands. Those same Parisians who had formed the Commune and nicknamed Thiers the "butcher".

When the Charrúas reached Paris, the Gare d'Orsay was not yet a museum, writers met in the Closerie des Lilas to drink absinthe, and decent people kept well clear of the Marais district after dark.

The Frenchman put them in one room in a cheap hotel. They spent hour after hour there, crying, talking in their own tongue. The Frenchman was decent enough: he bought Guyunusa a straw hat and parasol, the men frock coats and walking sticks. But they just stared at him in a sad, distant way, not daring to leave their room, where the light never ceased to shine. In this strange place, they were frightened of the night. He couldn't understand it: hadn't he saved them from a terrible fate, from being shot or shut in prison for the rest of their lives? All he asked was for them to show willing. If they never looked happy, who would want to go and see them? They were already contracted to appear in various local fairs, and in a quite well-known circus. Ivry-sur-Seine, Aubervilliers, Montrouge. A poster was made showing Tacuabé, his face painted and wearing feathers as if he were in mourning for a relative. "They were in mourning for all their relatives, for the grandfathers of their grandfathers, who groaned and sighed in the air around them. The whole world was poorer without them."

Professor Leclerc did not want to read any more. The museum had paid two thousand francs for the mummies of the indians, who had never adapted to the Parisian climate. A bout of influenza finished off Guyunusa, and the others followed soon after, lacking the will to live. They had never been a big attraction in the suburban fairs, no match for the spiderwoman or the tame bear. An accommodating taxidermist dealt with them as though they were exotic birds. They were put on show in the "Objets Divers" room, but after a while began to lose their hair and to be attacked by moths. The embassy of the country they came from sent a delegation to the museum to recover them and take them home for an exhibition that celebrated the history of the republic. But the museum refused, arguing that they were of scientific interest and that it would be dangerous to set a precedent in such a sensitive area. What if the Greeks were to ask for the Parthenon sculptures, saved by Lord Elgin from being blown up with the rest of the temple when the Turks turned it into an arsenal? What if Egypt claimed back the bodies of its pharaohs, the statues of its princes? No, the question of all the treasures of the past which now belonged to the world's great museums was an intractable one.

In more recent times it had been the indigenous groups themselves who claimed the bones of their ancestors, and the museum had been forced to employ teams of lawyers to defend itself in lawsuits and tribunals. The museum argued that these organizations had no right to claim any remains or bones of groups with whom they had no direct blood relation. But the vast majority of the skeletons the museum owned belonged to now extinct groups and tribes. The museum also claimed it had no more than a few score moth-eaten mummies and fragments of bodies, from a wide range of historic periods.

The nightmares are not so insistent now, but I still feel uneasy, as if something or someone were asking something of me. Why should I be concerned about a heap of anonymous bones that are only of interest to a tiny group of fundamentalist fanatics?

Perhaps it's because I think of my own bones, and those of my parents and grandparents, and our family plot in the cemetery, which we always look after, take flowers to, go and pray over. I would not want some future archaeologist to examine them in order to determine from the width of my shoulderblades how tall man in the late 20th century was, or to take away my jawbone to see how many crowns or bridges I had, if they were made of amalgam or gold.

His father paid him an unexpected visit. They had a coffee in the museum restaurant overlooking the Champ de Mars. At that time of the morning there were no more than a dozen or so visitors in the museum, gazing at a dwelling that floated on the surface of a lake like a raft. The book his father had brought showed a flat country, with no mountains or forests. A country of wild, deserted beaches, sand-dunes and pines, weeping willows. A vast green and fertile plain full of cattle and sheep: this was the habitat of those sad, moth-eaten mummies who were calling out to him from the museum storeroom. The book was practically useless, with poor photographs and a leaden text that described at great length the natural charms of the country, its prairies, its wonderful meat, its capital city that was comparable to anywhere in Europe, thanks to its clean streets and great variety of cinemas and theatres. The divine Sarah had acted in the main theatre, and Caruso had woken the roosters when he sang Idamante in *Idomeneo*. It seemed to François that the mummies would feel as foreign in those streets as they had done in Paris a century earlier. The city seemed to want to forget its past as a port that offered a welcome to all the disinherited and persecuted, a port that had been the last outpost of whale hunting.

Yet that was their country, that was where they belonged and where they should be.

It wasn't difficult for him to get a key to the store after all: his job was to classify, catalogue.

The museum was a huge black block in the night, made even larger by his fear. He went in by a side door, avoiding the front entrance which was guarded by an infrared system that picked up any movement. The museum contained gold objects and priceless jewels. The walk to the store seemed longer than ever. He almost knew the way by heart, and found his way by the glow from the exhibits in their cases: bones that shone like ivory in the moonlight, blue feathers and red cloth that kept the memory of when they had been the accoutrements of a high priest, his obsidian knife plunging avidly. Te Tapuntzil, he who smells of rottenness.

The nineteenth-century case was easy to open. The packages were small: with the passage of time all that was left of the once ferocious warriors were these shapeless bundles in their yellowed canvas wrappings.

He put them in his sailor's bag, and heaved it onto his shoulder. On his way back he stumbled against several cupboards and shelves. The city was sleeping like a huge snake that had swallowed its prey, jaws at full stretch to cope with the head.

His apartment was quite close to the museum, but the walk up five flights of stairs left him sweating. That was the first night in several months that he had no nightmares.

He called up the museum and asked for a fortnight's holiday. He went to a travel agency to buy a plane ticket to South America. Before leaving he went to say goodbye to his father, who wished him luck. The mummies were duly packed in his equipment as "archaeological tools".

In the airport he felt quite safe. It would be at least five years before anyone in the museum discovered that the mummies had disappeared.

It was a long air journey, but he was used to travelling. He thought of the indians and their trip, the gigantic canoe which had taken them across the wide, wide river that the white men called an "ocean". Now they were undertaking a second journey, back to the seed, back to the roots they had been torn from. He slept and dreamt of the city he was headed for, which had suddenly become just as it had been in its early days, a place of ragpickers and soldiers, where salt and leather needles were worth their weight in gold.

The airport seemed to date from those days. His crates passed under the sleepy eyes of the customs police without much discussion: their seals made them look imposing. Several taxi drivers were disputing over a handful of tourists; François thought that in other times his bundles would have been received with pomp, speeches, an official cavalcade, flags fluttering in the breeze. If the delegation that had gone to reclaim them had succeeded, it would have been different again: the ambassador would have been made a minister in recognition of his negotiating skills, groups of patriots would have pointed out that this was a historic day, a day of welcome for these original inhabitants of the country, who had baptized it with the name of river of birds, place of shells.

Today though there was nobody to receive them. Nobody to cover themselves in glory with hypocritical appeals to the past: wasn't it the grandfathers of those same patriots who had hunted the indians down like animals along gullies and through the scrublands? It was they who had sold them, though now they claimed them as the founders of the nation.

François asked the taxi driver to take him to a beach where there wouldn't be many people. His lack of knowledge of the language made his request sound odd, but the driver was used to the whims of tourists. He left him at a beach surrounded by sand dunes and eucalyptus trees. He had taken the precaution of packing a spade and pick in his equipment. The earth was soft, so it took him no time at all to dig a deep hole. He was sorry that the indians had left no indication of exactly how they buried their dead, if they sang or wept over them. He knew only that the women cut off the knuckles of their fingers and painted their faces as a sign of mourning. For lack of any other ritual, he said a prayer to the lord of all men, the one who had said that everyone should follow him, Jews and gentiles, the one who had wanted to save everyone, righteous and sinners alike, indians and Pharisees, fallen women and Roman centurions.

He trod down the earth of the tomb for some time, until even he could not distinguish which patch of ground it was. Then he walked back up towards the road, hoping to find a car that would take him back to the airport.

Translated by Nick Caistor

Warning

Ariel Dorfman

For Saul Landau

*T*hat morning as usual, the caretaker opened the front door to the building. Then he pinned up the notice about the conference on the Mapuche indians at twelve, and went back inside. He didn't spot the paper bag.

Samuel Fuller, the director of the institute, would have seen it straightaway. But that morning as ever he had come in by the back door, and so it was only a half hour later while he was talking on the phone that he noticed out of the corner of his eye that there was a bag down by the front doorstep. It was his fifth phone call of the morning. The first had been to ask his daughter — whom he had left only twenty minutes earlier with a raging flu — if her grandmother had arrived to look after her. She had not. His second call had come as a relief: the grandmother did not answer at her own place, so she must be on the way and had obviously got caught up in the dreadful morning traffic. The third call reassured him that the interpreter had gone to pick up the Mapuche speaker as agreed, and that the two of them were on their way to the institute. The next one brought confirmation that a famous anthropologist would be there at twelve, and that he had promised to bring along an Associated Press corres-pondent he knew. And when Fuller spotted the grocery bag, he was in the middle of talking to a friend of his who was a journalist on the *Post*.

"You've got to come," Fuller was saying. "Nobody gives a damn what happens to these people. They're being wiped out, and nobody gives a sweet damn."

It was at that very moment that his eyes took in the paper bag. He could hear his own voice in the distance insisting — as it had done over the past year for a wide range of important causes — that of course Gloria had been particularly concerned about these matters. He didn't much care to hear himself talk like that, not because it wasn't true, but because it had become the echo of something he felt more profoundly, a ritual he took part in only reluctantly, out of a need that Gloria herself would have been the first to recognize, but in which her presence was gradually being eroded by this daily taking her name in vain. Yet Fuller continued: "You know her work was directly related to this question of the rights of indigenous peoples. And not just in Chile. In all Latin America. And here too."

But instead of really thinking about Gloria or the indians or how essential it was for the press to report on these matters, Fuller caught himself wondering whether his fridge wasn't dangerously and irresponsibly empty, and whether he shouldn't stop by at the supermarket on the way home that afternoon and fill several thick rough brown paper bags like the one down there with food for the week. For the next ten minutes, while he was busy convincing the *Post* journalist that it really was essential for him to come this time — come and bring a photographer with him as well — he kept staring at the bag. It was fascinating to see how the shoes of the members of the institute passed so close to the bag that they almost brushed against it, but none stopped for a single moment, none showed the slightest curiosity about what it contained. Of course it was a perfectly innocent-looking bag, similar to so much other rubbish the city deposited on its sidewalks, probably the legacy from some drunk or other the night before. A perfectly innocent object, apart from a slight bulge, what looked like a small hump on one side of the bag. When Fuller hung up this time, his eyes rested briefly, fleetingly, on Gloria's photograph that stood as always on his desk. A thought flitted across his mind, and he almost called his daughter again, but he managed to resist the temptation and went over to the window instead.

On the second floor of the building opposite, which was still blocking out the sun like a huge grey wall, an elderly couple were staring down into the street. Four years earlier, when Fuller first moved into this office after he got back from the southern cone of Latin America, the two pensioners had been in that very same spot, their armchairs and their steady gaze already a silent, permanent feature of this unaltering city landscape. They would spend the whole morning like that, quietly basking in each other's company. Sitting so close together they looked like a single breathing creature. Now they were there, watching the bag that no one had touched in the whole morning. Also keeping his eyes glued to it, as if watching a dangerous animal that might escape or leap at any second, Fuller groped for the telephone directory. This wasn't the first time he felt how absurd it was to be playing a role better suited to a second rate hero in some TV thriller series. A few months earlier he had anxiously scrawled the number of the local police station on the phone book cover. But this time he didn't dial. After a moment's hesitation, he decided to calm his pounding heart by going down first to see for himself. After all, there was no point making a fuss over nothing.

Over nothing?

In the bag were two chickens.

Not frozen chickens, the sort ready to roast, fry or throw into the pot. Chickens that are bought still alive in the countryside, chickens that someone has to pluck, then remove the innards with a knife, chickens whose yellow scraggy skin has to be singed slowly over a low fire. Chickens that can't be bought that easily in a city like Washington.

Someone had slit their throats.

"*Kallco*," a hearty voice said behind him, a voice he knew.

He turned round.

"*Kallco*," the Mapuche repeated.

Fuller shook the bag so that the two chickens would flop back in. So that neither he nor anyone else had to touch them again. But the crop of one of them refused to budge, as if it were stuck with glue to the serrated edge of the brown paper.

"*Buenos días, compañero*," Fuller said, while with a last rough shake of his hand he managed to force the chicken back into the bottom of the bag. He carefully deposited it in the same spot it had occupied all morning, next to the front door of the building. "Excuse me for not shaking hands, *compañero*, but . . ." Fuller pulled out a handkerchief and openly wiped his fingers clean.

"Witchcraft, *compañero*," the Mapuche said. "*Kallco*".

"Witchcraft?"

"In my country they do this to hurt people. They put something on the threshold so that things will go badly, so that someone will die or fall ill. They say that whoever goes in by that entrance will suffer."

The director looked down at his handkerchief. "We have to call the police," he said.

"The police?" the Mapuche queried. "What for?"

"We have to," Fuller said, "right now."

The first policeman scratched his head. "A report?" he asked. "I don't see anything that needs reporting."

"Yes, a report," Fuller insisted. "The institute demands one. So that we have written proof if something terrible happens later on."

"Something terrible? Could you please tell me just what terrible event these two chickens are threatening?"

"The death of two people," Fuller said. "Isn't that enough for you? Two members of this institute were . . ."

The phone rang.

"It's your daughter, Mr Fuller. Shall I put her through?"

Her grandmother had still not arrived. Fuller glanced at his watch. It was ten o'clock.

"Look, my love," Fuller said, conscious of the pause between each word. He turned his back on the others in the room and suddenly again saw the building opposite, the old couple, the traffic in the street, the entrance to the institute. "I can't do anything right now. I've got some business to attend to . . . no, it's nothing serious . . . what's wrong with my voice? No, really, there's nothing wrong, little one. If granny hasn't arrived by eleven, leave a message with Rachel and I'll send someone to be there with you, OK?"

When he turned back to face the policeman, his expression was firm and determined.

"We therefore consider this incident," he said, as though there had been no interruption at all, "as a further instance of the growing campaign against those of us who work in this institution. We won't leave the Latin American dictatorships in peace, so the agents of those dictatorships . . ."

He could tell from the bored look in the policeman's eyes that this line of reasoning would get him nowhere. So he said: "What I'm trying to tell you is that there has been a sustained campaign against us. Threats, slanderous attacks, just like the last time."

"Could I say something here?" the policeman put in. "There's a big difference between killing a chicken and killing a human being. I'm not aware of any law that's being broken in this particular case."

In reply, Fuller allowed a note of exasperation to creep into his voice. He added to the effect by shooting out his clenched white fists across the desk top. "I for one am perfectly aware of the difference between a chicken and a human being. You can save your wisecracks for when you are off duty, officer."

The policeman poked at the offending object with the tip of his boot. "I didn't mean any disrespect, Mr Fuller, but as I see it, someone forgot their bag of shopping. That's all there is to it."

"Allow me to remind you," the director said, "that this gentleman is a member of the Mapuche nation from Chile. In his country, an act of this kind is regarded as a death threat."

"And allow me to repeat," the policeman retorted, "that we are not in Chile, but in Washington DC, which happens to be the capital of the United States of America. And that, according to our laws . . . well, to tell the truth, I wouldn't even know where to file your complaint, what category to put it under."

"What did he say?" the Mapuche asked the interpreter.

"That the chickens are out," the interpreter whispered. "He doesn't want to write a report."

"All this nonsense," the Mapuche said. "But this is your country, you know best."

The second policeman, a sergeant, arrived half an hour later to take over. He wouldn't commit himself either.

"My colleague was right. If I accept this complaint, they'll think I've gone crazy." He took a deep breath. "Can you tell me what public nuisance, what crime . . ."

"Threats," the director cut in.

"Threats? But there's nothing written down, there's been no phone call. No names either. How are we supposed to know who this . . . this . . . is aimed at?"

"In the Mapuche culture," the director said slowly, stressing every word, "this is like a telegram. They don't need to write the threat down. All they have to do is slit the gullet of a couple of chickens."

"Sounds like a big waste of food to me," the sergeant said. "A written note would be much more effective."

He looked at the bag with distaste.

"What did he say?" the Mapuche wanted to know.

"That it's a shame to waste food like that."

"He's right," the Mapuche said. "It is a shame. That's why they do it. To very poor people, sacrificing two chickens to frighten someone — well, what could be a more serious threat?"

"He is explaining," the interpreter said, "that the people of his land have limited resources and therefore if someone goes to the trouble of killing two valuable animals, there must be a lot of hatred."

"That may be true down there," the sergeant said, "but up here I have no authority to put anything like that in a report."

"You leave me no alternative," Fuller said, "but to call in one of your superiors."

"Go right ahead," the sergeant said. "It's a free country, after all."

"What did he say?"

"That this is a free country."

The third policeman turned out to be a lieutenant.

"So this gentleman is an indian, is he?"

"A Mapuche."

"And what is he here for?"

"He has come to denounce the fact," Fuller replied, "that in his country their land is being stolen from them bit by bit; their communal ownership of the land is being destroyed. And that since for his people the land is sacred and is what gives meaning and structure to all that they do, that is tantamount to genocide."

The lieutenant didn't say a word, so Fuller went on. "Just like what happened here."

"Here?" the lieutenant asked. "Where?"

"Here," the director said, "in the United States."

"Nothing like what you've just been describing ever happened here in the United States," the lieutenant said.

"What's he saying?" the Mapuche wanted to know.

"Rubbish," the interpreter said.

"You find these practices," the lieutenant continued, "in many religions. The sacrifice of poultry, I mean. In the Caribbean, in Haiti for example. Or in Central America, and among some Mexicans. This gentleman here has no reason to feel it is directed against him. Even if we accepted the meaning of these chickens, even with that hypothesis, there is no proof that this is meant against him personally."

"In the ten years since this institute was founded," Fuller said, raising his voice, "we have never once found a dead chicken in our doorway. Dead people, yes. But never a dead chicken. Are you really going to tell me it's a coincidence that just a few hours before . . .?"

"If we spent all our time looking for everyone who kills a chicken, sir, we'd have none left for people who rob and kill."

"It is my dearest wish," Fuller said, "that you spend all the time in the world searching for people who kill. As you are well aware, I have my own reasons for wishing you every success in that task. But I don't think you quite understand what we are asking you for here. Neither my friend nor any of us wants a bodyguard. We simply want our complaint to be registered in an official report."

"I'd ask you to calm down, sir, if you please."

"I'm perfectly calm."

"I wouldn't say that you're calm." The lieutenant looked over at the interpreter. "Would you say that this gentleman is calm?"

The interpreter opened his mouth to say something, then thought better of it.

"Lieutenant," Fuller said, "the institute would prefer to keep quiet about this incident. But if you force me to bring it out into the open, at noon today we expect to have a room full of journalists in this very building . . ."

"I don't think they'd make much of it," the policeman said. "But in this country you never know. If you insist, let's be going downstairs."

"What for?"

"So that I can take your statement on the spot, Mr Fuller. Isn't that what you want?"

"I don't see any need to go downstairs," Fuller said.

"Listen, I won't teach you how to defend Latin Americans or indians," the lieutenant said, "and you don't teach me how to take statements. Agreed?"

Downstairs, in front of the building, the lieutenant put the parcel with the two chickens back on the doorstep.

"Is that how it was first thing this morning?" he asked the caretaker.

"I don't recall," the caretaker replied. "I didn't pay it any attention."

"Yes, that's how it was," Fuller said. "I found it there. But I still don't see why it is so important . . ."

He looked up and, above and beyond the policeman, he could make out the old couple on the second floor of the building opposite. They had stood up to get a better view of the scene below. For a split second, he was fascinated by the man and woman studying what was going on from behind their window-panes, so welded together it seemed they had spent the last eighty years in the same position, knowing right from the start that nothing and nobody could ever separate them.

"OK," the lieutenant said, "ask the indian gentleman who he suspects."

"He only arrived last night," the interpreter said. "He doesn't know a soul in the city."

"Do you want a report or not? Ask him."

"We could check," the Mapuche said, "to see if there are any other Mapuches in Washington."

"We'd better not say that," the interpreter decided. "They don't have that kind of information. They'd think it was a personal or tribal matter. Or maybe even a fight over a woman."

"Whatever you say," the Mapuche agreed. "But it must have been another Mapuche. Just think, coming all this way to do something like that here . . ."

"What's he saying?" the lieutenant wanted to know.

"He's thinking about it."

"Something that shows the political nature of the threat," Fuller said in Spanish, his eyes still fixed on the couple in the building opposite.

"If I accuse my country's military government without any concrete proof," the Mapuche said, "they might take away my passport and I wouldn't be able to go home. We'd better tell him we have no idea who did it."

"He doesn't accuse anyone of being behind it," the interpreter said.

"Does he have any suspicions?"

Without waiting for a translation of the question, the Mapuche said: "The people who want to stop me giving my talk."

The lieutenant scribbled a jumble of words in his notebook, then stared down at the bag again. "And is he going to give his talk anyway?"

"He's asking if we're going to continue with the talk, *compañero*."

For the first time that morning, a smile spread across the big round face tanned by the sun of southern Chile.

"Tell him we're not scared of live chickens, so why should we be frightened of dead ones?"

The policeman stopped writing. He could sense that some bystanders had begun to gather behind his back.

"If you're not frightened," he said in a voice that boomed out over the tiny group standing round the doorstep, "then why are you making this complaint?"

Fuller found himself obliged to turn his attention away from the old couple on the second floor and stared directly at the lieutenant. "Since when," he said, almost in a whisper, almost disguising the savage irony of his words, "is it necessary for the victim to be afraid for a threat to exist? Or for there to be a murder?"

"Have it your own way," the lieutenant conceded, "you can see I'm writing down the whole of this goddam affair. I'm going to classify it under miscellaneous, there's room for anything and everything there."

The others watched the even flow of his pen across paper for a minute or more. Anticipating action, the spectators on the sidewalk pressed closer to try to catch the final exchanges. At last the pen came to a halt. "Ask him if he has any further statement to make."

The Mapuche studied the three or four passers-by who had stopped to watch, as well as the members of the institute who had joined the group. They were all casting him sideways glances as if they were a long way away on that warm autumn day in Washington.

"I've nothing more to say to him, but when he's gone, there's something I'd like to say to you two, if that's all right."

And five minutes later, when he, Fuller and the interpreter were on their own again in the office:

"I'm sorry, my friends, but I don't think any of that was necessary."

"It's not the first time we've received threats," the director said.

"And the last time . . ." the interpreter said.

There was a long silence. "And the last time . . .?" the Mapuche wanted to know.

"We ignored it," Fuller said. "That's why this time we want a proper report of everything. So that they know we realize what they're up to."

"I can understand that, *compañeros*. And I can see that it's useful for you to do that. But as far as this threat is concerned, my mind's more at ease now than when I woke up this morning."

"More at ease?"

"Those people must be really scared if they have to turn to witchcraft. Just think, *compañero* Fuller. They have the weapons, they have the laws, they have the judges, they have the money for loans. What else do they have that I'm forgetting? Ah yes . . . the banks, books."

"The newspapers," the interpreter said, "the television."

"The newspapers, the television. They have everything. And they say there are no indians. That we do not exist. The other day they diverted the water from one of our communities, they simply stole it, and when the Mapuche went to make a complaint, we were told we should hire a lawyer. For them we are no longer Mapuche, we are only individuals. There are no laws to protect us. And since we can't afford a lawyer, the community will have to sell land. To the same white neighbour who stole our water in the first place. But I'm less worried now."

Fuller sat on the edge of his desk and stared out of the window. Down below, the lieutenant was picking up the bag with the chickens and putting it into a police car that was waiting for him, its red lights flashing. He could feel the twin pairs of eyes in the building opposite following the car until it turned the corner.

"I'm sorry, *compañero*," Fuller suddenly said, still gazing out at the street. "I seem to be having difficulty understanding things today. I don't see why you aren't worried. Things like this really make me upset . . . too upset, perhaps."

"But it's obvious. According to them, we don't exist. Yet they have to use a custom of ours, of my people: they have to resort to killing two chickens in the capital of the United States of America, no less. And all to try to stop me speaking."

All of a sudden, the eyes of the old couple swivelled to focus directly on Fuller. Then they stepped back from the window, and an unseen hand slowly drew their curtain. Fuller imagined them in the kitchen preparing a light lunch, imagined them getting ready to take a good nap. He took off his glasses and turned to look, acutely conscious of how blue his Yankee eyes were, at the man standing calmly on the other side of his desk.

"Do you mind if I ask you a personal question? This chicken thing. Do you believe in it? In the power of witchcraft, of curses? That we can tell when something terrible is about to happen to us? In all that sort of stuff?"

"In my land," the Mapuche said, "the people believe it. What I myself think does not matter."

"I must confess to you," Fuller replied, "that I can't take these things lightly. They make me nervous. Ever since . . . well, since a year ago I see every incident like this as a warning that something dreadful is about to happen."

"As if someone were watching you," the interpreter suddenly suggested.

"As if someone were watching me," Fuller agreed.

The phone rang.

It was Fuller's daughter. Her grandmother had just arrived. She had taken so long because she had decided to go and buy a special treat for her sick granddaughter and for Fuller. So they wanted to know whether he was going to eat at home with them that evening.

When he hung up, Fuller felt that he ought to give some explanation.

"My daughter woke up feeling ill," he said. "I think you're going to have to excuse us from the dinner we had planned for tonight. Her grandmother is looking after her, but I don't know if . . . as you know perhaps, my wife . . ."

He gesticulated in the vague direction of the portrait on his desk, then towards the street, from where they could hear the constant rumble of traffic.

The Mapuche closed his eyes for a moment.

"I know, *compañero*. I heard about it. You can't imagine how sorry we all felt."

Fuller put his glasses on again and looked at his watch.

"Well, well. It'll soon be time for the talk . . . but please, you were telling me something when they rang. Please . . ."

"It's nothing. It's just that those people must feel very weak, that's all. They must be very desperate if they have to turn to our own culture to try to frighten us, to use such extreme measures."

At that instant, the first ray of morning sunshine shone from behind the building opposite, streaming in through the office window like a cockcrow of light.

Fuller blinked and shaded his eyes.

"You think so, *compañero*?" he asked slowly, choosing his words carefully, and going over to take the Mapuche by the arm. "You think so? Because as I see it, they're strong. Very strong."

"Very desperate," said the Mapuche.

Translated by Nick Caistor

Three Days

Luisa Valenzuela

To Maxine, who told me this true story;
to Doug Boyd for the quotes from Rolling Thunder

*R*olling Thunder quit our Institute for Psychophysical Research, slamming a metaphorical door when he discovered someone had been tampering with his healing feathers. He left, and the worst storm ever seen in northern California immediately began. It blew off roofs, toppled trees, and two huge eucalyptus fell across the driveways to the institute, leaving us cut off from the outside world, unable to get out.

But we knew there had been a gap of three days.

We took the feathers on the Tuesday afternoon. Rolling Thunder left on Friday, as if he had only just discovered the outrage. Was he waiting for the storm? If so, he was the only one who knew it was coming, because the weather forecasts never so much as mentioned the possibility.

Even so, to foretell something is very different from creating it.

Before the catastrophe happened, all anyone in the Institute could talk about was Rolling Thunder's power, though he was as unforthcoming about it as all his tribe are. He talked about healing but hardly ever unwrapped the feathers themselves.

He would gather us all round him in a circle on the lawn, and explain that the feathers were used for healing, and did just that, but that we shouldn't even begin to dream of using them; we had no right to think about our own health before we had tried to heal the world, the universe. How can you possibly heal yourselves of the sickness you carry around with you when you are busy making mother Earth sicker by the day, polluting her, eroding her, stripping her of her own creatures while you fill her with horrors, with cities, factories, nuclear power stations, superhighways? "We indians are the keepers of the land," he would tell us over and over. "We don't claim we own the land, because nobody can own it. The land belongs to the Great Spirit, but it has been delegated to us. We are the keepers of the land. Wherever you go on this planet, if there are any indians left, any survivors at all, there will be those among the original people who know the laws of life, of land and air. That is our mission, just like other men have been entrusted with other tasks. We all have to work together to make life good for all of us who live upon this mother Earth."

We drank in his words, even though we were sceptical at times. Rolling Thunder insisted: "Nature is sovereign and man's inner nature is sovereign too. Nature is to be respected. All life, every single living being, is to be respected. That is the only answer."

Then he would go on to attack the felling of trees on the reservation, the attempt to dump toxic waste there, or the pollution of the waters. We all wanted to hear more about healing and feathers, something useful, something we could put into practice to show we hadn't been wasting our time listening to him. That is why we replied with a sigh, as if apologizing: There's no stopping progress.

Progress? Rolling Thunder queried in disbelief. He always responded to our assertions with a question. All he deigned to tell us about his feathers was how they hunted the eagle, the respect they felt for the bird which was to provide them with the feathers, its ritual death and then how the feathers were prepared, how they got their healing power.

We listened to him quite enthralled, until Keith suddenly caught this goddam fever. We knew what was wrong with him, the doctors said there was no hope, but we thought we could offer him some.

We asked Rolling Thunder, we begged him, implored him.

We wanted to try out what we'd learned, to be able at last to display our powers. Rolling Thunder had taught us the basics of the ceremony, its essence, now we were being offered a unique opportunity to put it to the test.

No, Rolling Thunder said. You can't do it, you are not from the race of feathers.

"What race? What race are you talking about?" we said. "We don't believe in races."

I'm talking about the race which keeps harmony, which doesn't destroy just for the sake of it. There is always a harmony, he said, there is always harmony. If we heal in one place, we cause illness in some other part of the universe. You have to learn to accept this idea. Those who do not understand this harmony, those who only bring sickness to the planet, cannot heal. He had more to say, but we wouldn't listen because we were desperate: we had a dying Keith on our hands, hands that held the power to save him.

"Every case of sickness and pain exists for a reason. (We wouldn't listen.) We know (said he, but we were thinking: he may know it, but we don't and we aren't interested anyway) that everything is the result of something else and in its turn causes something else, and this goes on like a chain. You can't just make the whole chain go away. Sometimes a certain sickness or pain is meant to be because it's the best possible price to pay for something: you make the sickness go away and the price becomes greater (what price is he talking about, when he always claims he isn't interested in things like that, we were thinking). That's why we always take three days to look into a case, to see if we'll take it or not. As people we may not know the answer, but the Spirit does, and tells us of it. That is the task of a true medicine man."

Give us some proof, a demonstration, we asked him.

I've got nothing to prove, this isn't a circus, he told us, then disappeared into the woods to meditate.

That was on Sunday. By Tuesday we couldn't stand it any longer: we had the healing power within our grasp, the power, the power to bring Keith back to life, the power to be Rolling Thunder, the power to be God.

While Rolling Thunder was away, we took his feathers.

We borrowed them, let's say, while Rolling Thunder — to wriggle out of responsibility, no doubt — spent the whole day meditating in the woods.

Keith was in a coma. We performed the ceremony as best we could. Rolling Thunder had explained it to us, in the abstract, like someone talking about another dimension or a reality he knew we could not share.

We created the holy space by smoking the pipe four times, facing the four cardinal points:

> To the East where the sun rises
> To the North where the cold comes from
> To the South where the light comes from
> To the West where the sun sets.
> To the father Sun
> To the mother Earth.

Then we set to work with the feathers over Keith's dying body.

That afternoon Keith stirred, turned on his side, breathed a sigh. He seemed to have passed from a coma to a deep, calm sleep. We quickly put the feathers back where we had found them. Rolling Thunder must be about to return from his meditation.

I insist that this was on Tuesday. Did it really take Rolling Thunder until Friday to realize we'd been using his blessed feathers?

Then he upped and left our institute in a rage, and a little later the blue, blue sky turned dark, the thunder started, a rolling sound in the distance that began to draw closer until the thunderclaps were preceded by flashes of lightning that seemed to crash right on top of us. Flashes like huge snakes of light.

That was how the famous storm was unleashed.

We'd like to believe Rolling Thunder somehow knew the storm was on its way and took advantage of it as Egyptian priests did of eclipses.

The storm was really terrifying. It shook the land, and the sea rose in waves that almost reached the top of the cliffs and swept us away. The trees were uprooted, one lightning bolt split the century-old eucalyptus which fell across the main entrance; moments later, another brought down the second one, trapping us between them. The road was impassable.

The phone was down, so was the radio. It took days for the rescue team to reach us. We weren't too worried: we are medicine men at last, we learnt and were able to apply perfectly all the secrets we had so grudgingly been offered. We have the power, thanks to which we carried out the first of our feats: Keith's fever disappeared completely. He's out of danger now, as his baffled doctors admit.

Translated by Nick Caistor

Slice of Life

Alfredo Bryce Echenique

*T*o start with the drab sun of Lima or at any rate the drab sunlight of that dusty afternoon in Lima in the middle of the celebrations to honour the black Christ with its overtones of moorish Andalusia mixed with a certain savour of mischievous negro in his purple cloak, descendant of the slaves we once had; that afternoon during a week of processions, a Sunday of bullfights in honour of Our Lord of Miracles in the Plaza de Acho, built by the viceroy Manuel Amat y Junyent, famous for his Peroonbeach, his bridge and the main avenue in Lima, you must have heard about the palace of the viceroy's wife from Barcelona, the one they called the Peruvian Pompadour or rather the Pompadour of Lima, Micaëla Villegas, yes the Pompadour from Lima, and some wiseguy also knew that there was written about that splendiferous woman of our americas who had the poor old viceroy by the horns he was so crazy about her, or so crazy about her pussy more like, Peruvian bitch he wanted to call her but being Catalan all he could manage was that Peroonbeach especially when she had cuckolded him and he got so jealous, no wonder he was a Field Marshal in Spain, governor of Chile and such a magnificent viceroy of Peru, yes Offenbach wrote a famous operetta about Peroonbeach which is still performed at the Châtelet in Paris, with Luis Mariano . . .

All this as they're driving through the dust, past the squalid hovels in the drab sunlight on this excuse for a freeway which took them from the fortunate, gleaming white neighbourhood of San Isidro (long live riches and our sons of bitches!) down to the Lima of yesteryear, as if they were on a one-way ticket right round the world, with all these shacks back-to-back and only one tap among them, full of riotous common people, the worst, the dregs, and the president of the republic, call him a president? president of what I'd like to know brother, balls to that I say he's nothing more than a jumped-up general who's the son of a chink with a ragged ass and as common as a recruit, have you heard now he's going on about land reform and worse still reckons we should drink Peruvian whisky thank god we can still get the proper smuggled stuff and what about that pisco sour at our hot and spicy Peroonbeach of a lunch today they're choosing the winner of the Golden Cape, it's between José Mari Manzanares and Paquirri . . .

And for the hundredth time, well away by now, they called him some kind of a homo for coming out with yet another French word but in fact what all his fine rich friends from school and university were really mad about was that he had said he was in favour of land reform the asshole, what about your own family's lands, what about the Huacho estate? Haven't they cut your balls off too, or have you gotten to be a complete maso over in that Paris of yours, brother . . .?

That word brother spoken with all the affection of school days, for old times' sake, always somehow defused the situation, but on that excuse for a freeway in the drab sunlight and now it was getting real late and shit hasn't this week's bullfighting been the worst for years, all because of that asshole chink who claims to be running the country when all he's doing is pissing it down the drain, thanks to him Peru doesn't have any dollars to bring decent bulls over from mother Spain anymore, so they have to pay the bullfighters in Peroonbeach silver, shit, we're in it up to our necks all right, brother, it's enough to make you quit the country out of shame, brother, but no you insisted that land reform was a must, for the good of the country, no less, did you hear what Javier said, gentlemen? Come on, get another shot down you Javier, at least pretend you're getting drunk, right, cousin of mine?

It's getting late, real late, get in the car we're off, look at the way they've ruined all this stretch, look at how filthy it all is, brother of mine, as soon as you leave San Isidro forget it, the rest is filth, brother, as soon as you try to build a freeway they go and fill it up with their shacks, look at those asshole indians they don't even know how to cross a road, what the fuck are they doing strolling across like that, step on it Lucho we've no time to lose, we've still got to find somewhere to park, why are you easing up? foot on the floor brother, drive straight at the stupid cameloid creature — knock him down, squash the bastard, reform his land for him, you'll see how shit pours out instead of blood, pass me that wineskin brother, step on it now, an indian's skin is worthless as that writer Ribeyro said, he's another one who's hopped it to Paris like you Javier, isn't he? Shit, you got him brother, just look at him go . . . nothing, you hardly touched him, asshole cameloid creature, look at him crawling off, foot on the floor, give it all you've got, we've still got to park, if we're not careful we'll miss the procession, I want to see bulls not llamas, brother of mine "we're the best-known kids of this fine and noble town, we're the bigshots that no one can ever put down" pass that wineskin will you? what's wrong with you Javier don't be such an asshole, what are you trying to do to us? All right have it your own way get out and look but it's your own funeral . . . "We're the life and soul of the party, we make the finest music, and if there's any fighting to be done, we're not ones to refuse it" yes go on get out if you must, shit . . .

And when he reached the cameloid creature there was only a trickle of blood coming from the nose and he thought thank god as he saw him get up and scuttle away scared stiff of me . . .

As usual, not many of them had come to see him off at the airport, apart from sometimes a girl like a parting gift from this horrible Lima, just as not many of them had come to meet him, sometimes perhaps one of his brothers, and of course no one was waiting for him at Paris airport either. A smell of closed rooms and inevitable return in his flat, the emptiness of a world left for ever, the troubling sense of a world never properly discovered. Tiredness from his journey only made him feel even more displaced, as he stared at the things Nadine had left with him when they had said goodbye in . . . he couldn't even remember where exactly he had said goodbye to Nadine seven months earlier he was for ever saying goodbye to Nadine for a long time or for ever thanks to that split personality of hers, her frigidity, her fear of living, her past which seemed to hang round her neck, condemning her although she was still so young, a good bit younger than him. Nadine and her incongruous letters, her silences, her periods of forgetting him completely, Nadine who had turned his seven months in Lima into torture, and to think his only reason for going there in the first place had been to find her a job as a tennis coach, and to find himself whatever job he could because, it was true, the land reform had made life difficult for him too, so what he had to do, no other solution as his brother had said, you'll have to find a job either in Paris or in Lima, depending on where you want to settle, I'll give you all the contacts you need, but I can't exactly see that Nadine fitting into our family can you Javier? so perhaps it would be better in Paris eh brother?

The person on the phone said sorry wrong number but he recognized how clumsy and embarrassed Nadine was even at dialling the wrong number, stuttering with emotion or embarrassment. Nadine who wanted to want him, and had probably been phoning for days, working out when he would be back, ashamed at not having been able to hold on, at having behaved so badly towards the man who had gone to Peru to find her a job as a tennis coach so they could start a new life together, a life free of that past of hers, which now they only managed to escape occasionally on a beach in Huelva when they would swim naked together, trying to reach tenderness even if there was no love although they so much wanted there to be, something they could share, something more than this constant desire to start all over again from the beginning, with all that had happened forgotten and forgiven, perhaps all that they needed to be able to live together was a total, permanent amnesia about the day before. The wrong number on the phone, because there were nothing but stutters of embarrassment and emotion. Poor Nadine.

He poured himself a stiff whisky so as to avoid answering the phone again and avoid feeling sorry for her because it had already rung about ten times and he had not answered it, so he sat in a doze like he always did after a trip like this, waiting for the night so he could take a sleeping pill and begin to come to terms with his jet lag. After three whiskies he did answer, his voice patient from tiredness, impatient to hear her voice. Why was he so taken with the metallic voice of a woman who could hardly ever get a word out, and when she did poured out a jumble of fear, embarrassment or emotion? It must have been his sense of tenderness, though at times it seemed to him more like a sense of pity for this beautiful woman who was so scared of absolutely everything and who would have loved, or rather needed — because Nadine was a coward and had nowhere else to go — to love him. Their conversation was not a success. On her side there was fear, embarrassment and emotion. On his at first a weariness at starting to build all over again on seven months of ruins, and his increasing weariness from the journey. By the end, because of his emotions too. He would go. He had known he would ever since he packed her presents in his suitcase back in Lima. Since before that, since he decided to pack them. Since before that, since the moment he began to buy them. Since before that, since the moment he decided to go and buy her presents. Since before that, since always. Nadine would be at Le Mans station, the train — she had already checked — left at ten in the morning yes from Montparnasse station, it took about three hours. She'd be waiting for him at the station and would take him on another sixty kilometres to a farm some friends of hers had.

Lots of kisses, poor Nadine, she seemed in awe of him, at the farm he'd be the hero just because he'd been in Peru, the jerks, he'd have to make up better stories than his rich friends complaining about land reform, it'd have to be Cuzco, Machu Picchu or better still cocaine and all the rest . . . jungles and hallucinogenic drugs. Throw in a wise man like Don Juanito as per Castañeda, *la petite fumée du diable*. And he'd have to dish out presents all around, the farm was full of children living in a natural state or in harmony with Nature or who had dropped out of the system or whatever shit they were into now. What makes it so awful, Javier thought, is to know all this before I even get there.

That was why he had taken wine and whisky. On the farm they smoked hash but did not drink. And now that he had dished out the presents he could start drinking his wine and accept some hash. Accept anything. He was still exhausted from the plane and from one of those nights after crossing the Atlantic plus the train journey to Le Mans then sixty snowy kilometres in a car that was falling to bits. Around six in the afternoon, the candles already lit, he began his stories. Fortunately he was interrupted at seven by the arrival of a tall thin guy with a face like a camel, something about his hook nose that suggested Arab blood, pockmarked cheeks and incredibly filthy, even filthier when he took off his olive-green anorak. When the newcomer went off to the bathroom Nadine became noticeably less affectionate towards Javier, as Jackie, a big round bundle of a man who was the only one on the farm that he really liked, whispered that the man was on the run. Drugs. From India. Jewels too.

So it all started up again when Nadine showed him, Yves his name was, the necklace with the huge green stone she'd just got from Peru. Yves asked Javier if he had any contacts in Brazil, and Javier replied that he only knew three estates in the Mato Grosso. Jealousy! Not that again, dear God. Or was it pity that he felt? Here we go again, anyway. Should he put up a fight or not? If he did, then it must be pity.

Fight he did for a while, using the cassettes he had brought from Lima so that he could tell Nadine about his experiences there: about the cameloid creature and the bullfight he never got to? About the wonderful flat his mother had found after his father died? How hard it had been to take flowers to his father's grave, how hard to arrive in Lima without a father for the first time, because he had not been able — no, had not wanted — to go back for his death? No, much better to translate the words of the songs for Nadine and stroke her naked body while she, every now and then, remembered to return his caresses, and was making an effort which he could tell was tremendous to stay with him, to stay with him this time, to stay with him this once because perhaps if she could manage just this once ... not to go. Not to let her head go.

All of a sudden Nadine told him she had seen a film she had liked a lot, and all through the film she had missed him dreadfully, it had really got to her. But then it turned out none of her friends had liked the film, for no particular reason, so she had been left not knowing what to think. It's a problem that bothers me a lot, Javier. Don't I have a mind of my own? It's horrible not knowing what to think. That's my problem Javier, I'd like to know what I think, like you do. When the cassette came to an end he stopped stroking her, he was too tired, it wasn't worth the effort of putting on the other side of seven months in Peru. He tried to caress her again, made a real effort, out of pity, but everything had become stale and flat. So he blew out the candle to make it easier for her to go and show her naked body to the newcomer. So she could drift away more easily, because she had no mind of her own.

At the agreed moment, Javier was thinking in the train on the way back to Paris, although the only thing he had agreed to was to go and see Nadine at the farm in contact with Nature, at the agreed moment the farm bathroom lay next to the bedroom where on the bed, at the agreed moment, Nadine lay naked and stiff while he waited for the agreed moment. Which wasn't long in coming because Yves, the black bristles of his hair curly with dirt, was running a bath. There was the sound of water, like the sound of an hourglass filling the emptiness of the bathtub and the terrible emptiness Javier felt when he contemplated the rout of the poor Peruvian hero in his battles of Machu Picchu, Cuzco, cocaine and a beautiful silver necklace with its huge green stone. Each and every battle lost to the superior forces of this agreed moment. Nadine's naked body stood up on the bed, avoided stepping on him, opened the bathroom door; a sliver of light pierced the bedroom, then it was plunged back into darkness as she closed the door behind her. It was not the moment to think that seven months in Lima trying to find her a job that would allow them to start a new life could end like this, in something he had known before he had even got there. All that Javier thought was that the new life must have been only for Nadine; his own life had been old for so long now, the same old same old life as ever.

The two of them were talking next door in the bathroom, but he didn't really want to know what about, then there was another flash of light in the bedroom as Nadine re-opened the door just as he was taking the sleeping pill of pity. Yves had asked her to ask him if the stone was real or if he had bought it in one of those ghastly tourist shops.

"Tell him," Javier said, "tell him that in Peru only Peruvians in the know and very rich tourists buy handicrafts and suchlike in the official tourist shops. It's your backpackers, your eternal tramps, the people who travel in charter planes and think they're off on a big adventure who buy the fake stones sold by the pedlars of 'authenticity'. Tell him I mean it, too."

Nadine closed the bedroom door again and back in the bathroom repeated her instructions as faithfully as she could, given that she had no mind of her own. Soon afterwards Javier fell into a deep sleep, pity, and the last thing that went through his mind was that in some book or other he had read that pity is one of the most terrible passions a human being can fall prey to. When he awoke he could hear breakfast noises; he grimaced at the thought of taking a bath in the same tub as Yves. It seemed as though Nadine had come back to bed at some point, there were signs of a furtive, naked return in the night, she had probably even woken up next to him, he could hear her voice now with the others at breakfast. Javier got up, packed for his journey back to

Paris, and as he was fastening the bag empty of presents looked out of the window and saw there was more snow than ever. Which made the trip from the farm to Le Mans station even more hazardous in the broken down old jalopy, and he didn't want to be harsh because Nadine had no mind of her own so he didn't ask her why when after breakfast and at the agreed moment for his departure he went to fetch his things from the bedroom he had found the huge stone from the necklace split in two, he didn't ask her how or why. Then it was all a rush because they hadn't expected so much snow, they arrived just in time at the station, he climbed aboard the crowded train while Nadine bought him a first class ticket then ran to hand it to him as the train was pulling out. Nadine who had said his only chance of a seat was in first class, who had shown great practical sense in organizing his hasty departure, who was this beautiful young woman running as far as she could along the platform blowing him goodbye kisses because she so much wanted to want him.

Javier arrived not once but over and over again, well at least three times: he felt he had arrived routed, exhausted, finished off, on at least three different occasions at Montparnasse station in Paris. He would have liked to be able to smile in the knowledge that he himself was living proof of the theory of relativity on top of his seven months' defeat in Lima and an honourable peace treaty signed on a farm for the defeated somewhere beyond Le Mans, he even told himself that all generals are wise once the battle is over, when all the idiots are dead. He also consoled himself with the thought that one is always someone else's cameloid creature, yet in spite of all his efforts, the incident in the train still seemed despicable.

He had been standing there thinking over all the agreed moment business when someone spotted that the conductor had come into the first class carriage. A woman stood up because she only had a second class ticket, and the person who had warned them asked who then did have the first class ticket. There were so many people standing up with only second class ones that at first Javier did not realize what he meant. But the man insisted so much that Javier finally took notice and remembered he did have a first class ticket and that in first class in France all the seats were reserved, so that must mean that the woman's seat was really his. He told her not to worry, it was all the same to him, but the conductor overheard and said that all those with first class seats should be sitting in them, ladies and gentlemen please, though in fact what he said was "diesgenmen" thanks to that economy of expression which certain languages permit, yes "diesgenmen" all those with second class tickets into second class please that means you too madam, hurry up please I've no time to waste. He checked Javier's ticket and told him yes that was his seat and he should sit in it because that was what he had paid for. Javier didn't even thank him — he was so aware that everybody was staring at him, all those who had turned round to watch the incident which Javier blamed on his absentmindedness over first class reservations and because his mind had been so busy with agreed moments.

But a man stood up as if this was another agreed moment and offered his seat to the woman who had taken Javier's while he was being so absentminded. Three more men followed suit, but the conductor insisted that second class to second class please, madam, and wouldn't take no for an answer, so conductor and madam fought their way to the next carriage while immediately there began a kind of chorus from the four men who had offered their seats in high dudgeon, plus a few short sharp comments from all those who had done nothing of the kind, and then what Javier a few moments later baptized as the silence of the silent majority. The pointed growls, the short sharp affirmations that almost sounded like someone aiming artillery, all agreed that there had been a time when there were third class compartments for third class people but nowadays *on n'est plus chez nous*, since when have foreigners travelled in first class, no, France isn't our home any more, diesgenmen, France isn't our home any more. That's basically what it was about and the silent majority and that cameloid creature who Lucho had run down on the Lima freeway only a few days earlier when he hadn't been able to take it and had got out and the cameloid had been so scared of me he had scuttled off, blood trickling from his nose. Javier instinctively raised his own hand to his nose, as if in a gesture of memory or of fear.

Now he was walking along the platform at Montparnasse station and the gentlemen with opinions plus the bombardiers who weren't at home any more either walked past him one by one, shooting him glances. You are the best-known kids of this fine and noble town, you are the bigshots who no one can ever put down. But he felt Paris was worth more than that, it was still the marvellous city where he and Sophie had loved each other so young, so wonderfully, in so privileged a way, with laughter, tears, the words immortal lovers use, still, the problem was this meant Lima was worth more than those who had once been his rich beloved friends at school and university and, although he thought he could spot a difference in the association-conclusion, it was too late and in Peru, in Lima, in the old-fashioned resort of Barranco, up beyond Lima's bridge of sighs, in the Embrujo restaurant, his brother had silenced the conversation to laugh at the presenter who was announcing La Limeñita and Ascoy, Rosita and Alejandro, who are honouring us, gentlemen, by leaving their immortal resting place to be with us once again, as always, as for centuries now, because Rosita and Alejandro, diesgenmen, already owed six months' rent when God announced *fiat lux*.

So while La Limeñita and Ascoy were helping him say goodbye to Lima with the waltz "Luis Pardo" about the famous bandit "come listen to my exploits, which were no more than heartaches," while Luis Pardo was calling on his enemies to kill him face-to-face, his brother Manuel was busy telling him he'd have to find some kind of job preferably in Paris, Javier, sorry but there's no place for that woman in our family, Javier began to applaud and couldn't stop himself, he would be leaving Lima soon so he got up and crossed the restaurant to give Rosita a kiss, tell her he had all her records in Paris, that he listened to them all the time. Rosita accepted his kiss graciously, said with emotion in her voice and a distinctly mortal look on her face, God bless you, you're a gentleman.

Translated by Nick Caistor

Axolotl

Julio Cortázar

*T*here was a time when I thought a lot about axolotl. I used to go and look at them in the aquarium at the Jardin des Plantes. I'd spend hours watching them, noting their immobility, their obscure movements. Now I am an axolotl.

Chance led me to them one spring morning when Paris was spreading its peacock tail after a long, tedious hibernation. I cycled down the boulevard Port-Royal, turned into St Marcel and L'Hôpital, saw the patches of green in among all the grey, and remembered the lions. I liked the lions and the panthers, but I had never ventured into the dank, dark building where the fish were housed. I propped my bicycle against the railings and began by looking at the tulips. The lions were sad and ugly, my panther was asleep. I glanced at a lot of ordinary-looking fish until by pure accident I came across the axolotl. I spent a whole hour gazing at them then left, with no eyes for anything else.

I looked them up in a dictionary at the Sainte-Geneviève library. I learnt that axolotl are the larval form, with external gills, of a family of salamanders called the Ambystoma. Before even reading the description on the card above their tank I had known they were Mexican, thanks to their tiny pink Aztec faces. I read that specimens have been found in Africa which can live on land during periods of drought and then return to live in water when the rainy season arrives. I found their Spanish name, *ajolote*, plus the information that they are edible and that their oil was used (apparently it isn't any more) like cod liver oil.

I didn't want to consult any specialist works, but went back the next day to the Jardin des Plantes. Soon I began going every morning, and sometimes the afternoon as well. The attendant gave me a puzzled smile as he took my ticket. I would lean on the iron rail that runs round the aquarium, and gaze at them. There is nothing odd in that, because right from the start I understood that we were linked, that something hopelessly lost and distant somehow still united us. I had known that from the moment when on that first morning I came to a halt in front of their glass-fronted tank, where air bubbles gently floated up from time to time. The axolotl were heaped on the cramped, sordid (only I can know just how cramped and sordid) floor of the tank, with its covering of stones and moss. There were nine specimens, ost of them with their heads pressed against the glass as they stared their golden-eyed stare at whoever came near. Uneasy, slightly ashamed of myself, I felt it was almost indecent to intrude upon those silent, motionless creatures piled at the bottom of their tank. I focused my attention on one of them, lying to the right and slightly apart from the rest, so that I could study it more carefully. I could distinguish a tiny, pinkish, almost translucent body (which reminded me of those Chinese statuettes made of milky crystal) like that of a small lizard some fifteen centimetres long, which ended in an extraordinarily delicate fish's tail, the most sensitive part of our body. A transparent fin ran the length of the body and merged with the tail, but above all it was the feet that fascinated me because they were so incredibly intricate, with tiny toes that ended in nails that were human down to the last detail. Then I discovered its eyes, its head. An inscrutable countenance, in which nothing stood out apart from the eyes, two holes no bigger than pinheads, a solid transparent gold in colour and totally lifeless yet staring, allowing themselves to be pierced by my own gaze, which seemed to penetrate this golden circle and plunge into a diaphanous inner mystery. The faintest of black haloes around the eyes defined them in the pink flesh, in the pink stone head that was roughly triangular in shape but had curved and uneven edges which made it look exactly like a timeworn statuette. The triangular shape of the head concealed the mouth, so that it was only from the side one could see just how big it was; from the front, it was a fissure that barely indented on the surface of the lifeless stone. On the sides of the head where the ears should have been grew three tiny reddish fronds like branches of coral, a plantlike growth that I suppose were its gills. This was the only part of the axolotl that showed any signs of life; every ten or fifteen seconds these fronds stiffened, then slowly drooped down again. Just occasionally, a foot stirred a fraction, and I could see the diminutive toes gripping the moss. We don't like to move around too much because the aquarium is so cramped; whenever we move, we bump into someone else's tail or head, and that causes problems, fights, weariness. Time is less of a burden if we stay quite still.

It was this stillness which led me to lean forward fascinated the very first time I saw the axolotl. In some strange way, I felt I understood their secret desire to abolish space and time through their apathetic immobility. Later I learnt better; the contraction of their gills, the groping of their delicate feet, their sudden swimming (some of them can swim with a simple wave movement of the body) proved for me that they were capable of escaping from the mineral torpor they spent hours caught up in. Above all, it was their eyes that obsessed me. Compared to them, the fish in the other tanks could only offer the boring banality of eyes that were beautiful like human ones. The axolotl eyes spoke to me of the existence of a different kind of life, another way of looking. I would press my face up against the glass (sometimes the attendant would clear his throat nervously) trying to get a better view of those tiny golden dots, the gateway to the infinitely slow and distant world of those pink creatures. It was no use rapping on the glass in front of their faces, there was never any noticeable reaction. The golden eyes just went on burning with that gentle, terrifying gleam of theirs; they went on staring at me from unfathomable depths that made my head spin.

Yet they were not that far away. I realized that long before things came to this, before I became an axolotl. I knew it the day I really came close to them for the first time. Contrary to what most people believe, a monkey's anthropomorphic features only serve to show what a vast difference there is between them and us. It was the complete lack of any such resemblance between axolotl and human beings which convinced me that my sense of oneness with them was real, not based on superficial comparisons. Only those minute feet of theirs . . . yet lizards also have similar feet, but there is nothing else they share with us. I think it was the axolotl's heads that settled it for me, that pink triangle with its tiny golden eyes. They looked and knew. They called out. They were not animals.

It seemed easy, almost too easy, to turn to mythology. I began to see in the axolotl a metamorphosis that could not entirely negate a mysterious humanity. I imagined them as conscious beings, trapped in their animal bodies, condemned for ever to the silence of the abyss, to their despairing introspection. Their blind stare, that tiny golden disc devoid of expression yet so incredibly lucid pierced me like a cry for help: "Save us, save us." I caught myself thinking up words of consolation, trying to convey a childish sense of hope. They sat there motionless all the while, staring out at me; then all of a sudden the pink fronds of their gills would stiffen. That produced a dull aching pain inside me: perhaps they could see me after all, could sense the effort I was making to penetrate the impenetrability of their lives. They were not human beings, but I had never sensed such a close tie with any other animal. The axolotl were like the witnesses of something, and sometimes like horrific judges. The terrifying purity of those transparent eyes of theirs made me feel unworthy. They were larvae; but the word larva can mean both mask and phantom. What image was biding its time behind those Aztec masks with their fixed inscrutability, their implacable cruelty?

I was afraid of them. I think that if I hadn't been aware of the presence of other visitors and the attendant, I wouldn't have dared stay on my own with them. "You gobble them up with your eyes," the attendant said, laughing. He must have thought I was a bit odd. What he didn't realize was that it was they who were slowly devouring me with their gaze, in an act of golden cannibalism. When I was away from the aquarium I could think of nothing but them, as if they exerted some kind of long-distance pull over me. I went to see them every day, and at night I dreamt about them, motionless in the darkness, then slowly stretching out a foot until it brushed against another one. Perhaps their eyes could see at night; perhaps for them day went on without end. Axolotl eyes have no lids.

I know now there was nothing strange in all this, that it was simply bound to happen. Every morning as I leaned towards their tank we were becoming more and more identified with each other. They were suffering, with every fibre of my body I could feel their pent-up suffering, the unyielding torture they went through on the floor of their tank. They were searching for something, some long-lost vanquished mastery, a time of freedom when the world had belonged to them. That fearsome look of theirs, so powerful it even forced its way through the lack of expression imposed on their stone faces, could only be conveying a message of suffering, a proof of their eternal damnation, of the liquid hell they were condemned to live in. It was no use my telling myself that it was my own sensibility projecting a non-existent consciousness onto the axolotl. We both knew otherwise. That is why there was nothing strange in what happened. My face was pressed against the tank as usual; my eyes were trying yet again to penetrate the mystery of those golden eyes that had no iris or pupil. Up close I could see the face of an axolotl immobile against the other side of the glass. With no transition, no sense of surprise, instead of the axolotl I saw my own face pressed against the glass, I saw it outside the tank, saw it on the other side of the glass. Then my face moved away, and I understood.

Only one thing was strange; to go on thinking just as before, to know. At first, becoming aware of this was like the horror of someone buried alive suddenly waking up to their fate. Outside, my face returned to the tank, I could see my lips pursing with the effort of trying to understand the axolotl. But I was an axolotl, and knew at once that no understanding was possible. He was outside the aquarium, his thoughts were thoughts outside the aquarium. Knowing him, being him, I was an axolotl, in my own world. The horror arose — I realized in a flash — from the belief that I was a prisoner in this axolotl body, transposed into it with my human way of thinking, buried alive in an axolotl, condemned to exist as a lucid being in the midst of all those stony creatures. But that fear vanished when a foot brushed my face, when I moved slightly to one side and saw an axolotl beside me staring at me. I realized it knew too; it had no way of telling me, but quite clearly it knew. Either I was inside it as well, or all of us thought like human beings, unable to express ourselves beyond the golden gleam of our eyes staring and staring at the face of the man pressed up against the tank.

At first, he came back often, but now he appears only seldom. Weeks go by without him showing up. I did see him yesterday though; he gazed at me for a long while, then suddenly left. It seemed to me he was no longer interested in us, that he was only there out of habit. Since all I ever do is think, I've been thinking a lot about him. I reckon that at first we were still connected, that somehow he felt more than ever linked to the mystery that obsessed him. But now the bridges between him and me are cut, because what was once his obsession is now an axolotl, remote from his life as a human being. I think at first I was able to keep in touch with him to some extent — only to some extent — and to keep alive his desire to know us better. Now I am for ever an axolotl, and if I think like a human being it is only because every axolotl thinks like a human being behind its pink stone image. I believe I was able to convey some of all this to him in the early days, when I was him still. And in this final isolation of mine, now that he never reappears, it comforts me to think that perhaps he is going to write about us, believing he is inventing a story that is going to write all this about axolotl.

Translated by Nick Caistor

Afterword: Two Anniversaries

Juan Goytisolo

*F*rance and Spain have commemorated on a grand scale two very different anniversaries which nevertheless share the fact that they mark decisive turning points in the history of their respective countries: the bicentenary of the French revolution in 1789, and the quincentenary of the Spanish discovery of the New World in 1492. Obviously events of the greatest importance, however much they may be criticized or attacked within the societies celebrating them, their current meaning and relevance need to be examined closely if we are to understand the range and significance of what is being commemorated.

If we think of the French bicentenary, all or almost all of us would agree in applauding an elected National Assembly representing the popular will, the abolition of the privileges of the nobility and the Church, the principles of liberty-equality-fraternity, the Universal Declaration of the Rights of Man and Citizen. However, historians and essayists who have reviewed the historical process begun in 1789 do not stop, logically enough, at the events of that year. Their examination of subsequent happenings provides a more cautious, sombre picture of the evolution and impact of the revolutionary process: Jacobinism and the dictatorship of a small revolutionary group, a precursor of twentieth-century Bolshevism; the Terror, and the guillotine with the *tricoteuses*; the Directory and its triumvirates; the Empire and the Napoleonic wars; the invasion of a continent in the name of liberating principles perverted by the megalomaniac ambition of a scheming officer crowned emperor for life by the Pope. Yet Napoleon's final defeat and the restoration of the Bourbon monarchy do not signal the ultimate failure of the revolutionary enterprise: despite the compromises and crimes, it did represent the beginning of a new era and its instrinsic values keep their force and universal validity today. The admirable Declaration of 4 August 1789 served and still serves as a weapon for colonized and oppressed peoples in their struggles against the colonizers and tyrants; it allowed and still allows all men and women without distinction of race or creed to have a legal defence against the whims of power and abuses of corruption. The French bicentenary in 1989 celebrated the generous aims of the representatives of the fourth estate, a set of principles that remains fully valid throughout the world in the fight against the lies and deceptions of churches old and new, one-party systems and their all-embracing "benefactors".

The commemoration of the quincentenary of the Spanish discovery of the New World offers a very different perspective. We must ask whether the values being celebrated can be said to be still both relevant and universally valid. The indigenous peoples of America who fell victim to the incursions and massacres of the conquest would quite rightly reject this idea: forced to work for their new masters, decimated by diseases the latter brought with them, dispossessed of their ancestral forms of government, culture and religion and sometimes driven like the Siboneys to collective suicide, they would not accept in any way the civilizing, dogmatic arguments used by the invaders. It would be ridiculous to deny the immeasurable importance of the conquest and with it the creation of Hispanic America: the fact that eighteen young nations play a role in the destiny of mankind, linked to Spain by a common past, culture and language. This whirlwind change in direction amid the complex social and administrative framework of empire may cause surprise and wonder, but to call this a "civilizing enterprise" — whether as a function of historical progress or of the salvation of heathen peoples — represents for the American indian societies of the time an obvious Eurocentric bias which denies them any values not based on Christian redemption or the imperatives of modern trade. In other words, the indians are judged not for what they themselves are, but in function of what they ought to be according to the premisses of an alien doctrine and social practice. The clear awareness of otherness, of the basic difference between what is ours (the virtues of civilization, the spreading of the Gospel) and what is theirs ("indians congregated in human herds", as Menendez Pidal would have it) justifies not only the condemnation of cultures that are distinct from our own but also their submission to the irrefutable arguments of those who, on behalf of their own criteria and values, wish to extend their rule over peoples who do not yet possess their ideological-religious view of the world. So as these other cultures are forced to pass through the hoop of our culture rather than simply remaining other and different, the well-intentioned ethnocentrist makes his appearance, striving to harness these strange, backward, exotic cultures to the great cavalcade of so-called material and spiritual progress, while lamenting the fact that innocent victims crushed by their juggernauts lie dying by the roadside.

It is true that in Spanish America the genocide of the indigenous populations was not as systematic as it was in North America: from Mexico to Chile, the conquest created the mixed societies we know today. The influence of Las Casas, Vitoria and other legal minds frequently moderated the abuses, and allowed a few fragile legal barriers to be erected to protect the indians, although these arrangements never applied to blacks, who continued to be the victims of slave trading until little more than a century ago.

Even, so, the ethnocentrism of the colonizing enterprise allowed no possibility for any ecumenical spirit: Spanish expansionism, endorsed by the historical mission of spreading the Gospel, was imposed by the sword without any respect for the wishes of the converted. That was doubtless common at the time: the age-old dichotomy between Greeks and Barbarians, the medieval one between Catholics and infidels, has persisted in a variety of guises well into the present century. But we are not seeking to apply criteria and ideas from today to past eras just to condemn the latter, but to determine whether there is anything to celebrate in the motives behind the awesome expansionism of the Spaniards.

If the values of the discovery and conquest cannot be seen as universal, can they be seen as valid and relevant to our own society and culture? The polemic unleashed in the sixteenth century by Las Casas (an exemplary attitude which is unrivalled in the history of all the other colonial adventures) focuses on the legal and moral bases behind the Spaniards' "historic mission". For Las Casas, the only credential that legitimized the Spanish irruption in the Americas was the papal bull giving them the right to do so. On the other hand, the defenders of the idea of the conquest as a "civilizing enterprise" have used a vast array of arguments, from the most noble, altruistic motives to other far more earthly ones. In his polemical essay "Insatiable Desire? Illustrious Deeds?" the historian Menendez Pidal writes how "the immensely spiritual soldier is also moved by a more personal kind of desire ... the desire for glory." The companions of Bernal Díaz del Castillo, our historian adds, died "so that in Mexico ... there would be master craftsmen printing books in Spanish and Latin; they died so that indians could learn to shape iron, weave silk, satin, taffeta and woollen cloth ... so they could carve and rival the works of Berruguete and Michelangelo." Can it have been for this alone? Menendez Pidal continues, "Naturally, the ordinary foot soldier was driven by other goals ... obviously, a soldier who risks his life daily for those 'who live in darkness' will be very wary when it comes to sharing out the gold that has been won." Quite so: and what about all the abuses, crimes, injustice? Menendez Pidal admits there were some of them in the Spanish colonization of America just as in the Roman colonization of the three Gauls. But wasn't the cruel Julius Caesar eloquently praised by Saint Augustine? Guatimocín perished in exactly the same way that Vercingetorix had been immolated. Why do the differences between these parallel lives matter? Menendez Pidal asks. In both cases, "the end was the same: *vae victis!*"

*

The double pull of evangelization and the thirst for gold did not come about as a consequence of the conquest. It was there right from the first. Significantly, on his return from the New World, Columbus addressed his first letters not to the Catholic monarchs but to the treasurers who had financed his expedition, mentioning the "possibility of rich earnings, and of establishing a flourishing slave trade". To Ferdinand and Isabel he wrote stressing "his exalted aim of converting the whole world to Catholicism" (W.T. Walsh: *Isabel the Crusader*). In 1494, Columbus sent four boats laden with slaves back to Seville to be sold on the slave market. The Catholic monarchs changed their minds about sanctioning the sale, and ordered they be freed and sent back to their country of origin. Unfortunately, as even Walsh points out, all the indians died of the cold before the Royal Order could be implemented. However, this is not the basic problem. Even if we discount these painful realities, we have to ask ourselves whether what are seen as the noble motives behind the conquest: "the attraction of achieving the impossible, of exceeding human resources", the "salvation of the indian hordes", the "desire for glory", the "search for heroic deeds" as Menéndez Pidal describes it, can be seen as present-day values. If we take into account the price paid by both indians and Spaniards, the answer must surely be no.

In the run-up to the quincentenary celebrations, Jorge Semprún and other politicians have been trying to disassociate the moment of discovery from that of the conquest in order to rescue the value of the former. In my opinion, as the correspondence between Columbus and Gabriel Sánchez proves, it is impossible to make such a separation. Can we honestly celebrate in our day and age any extraordinary human and technical feat of prowess independently of the historical context in which it is produced? Can we for example commemorate Gagarin's achievement without considering the economic, social, cultural and moral price exacted from the Soviet people by the Communist regime? Commemorate the feats of the incomparable Romanian athletes and swimmers while ignoring

Ceauşescu's despotism and megalomania, his wanton destruction of his country's historical heritage or the revolutionary launch of Germany's first car for the people while forgetting that it was produced by the Nazis? Despite the huge differences between these examples, there is one all-important connection: they are all created by closed societies cemented by a political or religious dogma used by the ruling orthodoxy to disguise all kinds of infamy.

A brief glance at the reign of Isabel of Castile will support my argument. As well as the undoubted successes of her administration that have been so enthusiastically detailed by Spanish historians, there was an important series of decisions and measures that prefigure the totalitarian states of modern times. These include the setting up of the Holy Office of the Inquisition with the aim of persecuting heretics and all those suspected of Judaism, a move which led to the use of *autos de fe* and the construction of public places for burning people at the stake; the decree expelling non-converted Jews announced on 30 March 1492 in the newly conquered Alhambra of the former kingdom of Granada; the creation of the Holy Brotherhood, the first state police force of modern times which, although established to control petty criminals, soon became infamous for its abuses and brutal methods which caused such an outcry in the main cities of Castile and Andalusia; the decree of 1497 that ordered the burning alive of all those found guilty of "heinous crimes against Nature"; the expulsion of "Egyptians and tinkers" (gypsies), on pain of a "hundred lashes and perpetual exile the first time, and the cutting off of their ears, sixty days in chains, and deportation if caught a second time"; the reneging on and subsequent repeal of the terms of the surrender of Granada, which expressly recognized the religious and cultural freedom of the Muslims; the burning of all Arab books and manuscripts on the orders of Archbishop Cisneros . . . I leave it to my readers to establish the parallels between what happened during Isabel's reign and what has taken place much more recently in other countries.

"A society defines itself not only in relation to the future, but also to the past," Octavio Paz has written: "its memories are no less revealing than its projects. Although we are worried by our past, we have no clear idea of what we have been. What is worse, we don't want to have one. We live between myth and negation, we deify certain periods and forget others. These forgotten areas are important: there is censorship of history as well as of the mind. Our history is a text full of passages written in black ink and others written in invisible ink. Paragraphs brimming with self-admiration, followed by paragraphs crossed out." Although Paz is here referring specifically to Mexicans, his remarks fit the Spaniards perfectly. The historiography of Isabel the Catholic is a history full of admiration and paragraphs crossed out. While it would be wrong to replace hagiographies like Walsh's with works that focus only on the mistakes and outrages of her reign, it did see the start of a truly lamentable process of uniformity. No other government has launched such an assault on public and private freedom, or on every kind of minority.

To conclude, let us compare the French bicentenary with its commemoration of the principles of political and individual freedom with our own Spanish quincentenary. The Spanish discovery of America was a gigantic technical and human feat which changed the course of history, but the values it embodies do not have the same contemporary relevance or ecumenical spirit. We cannot celebrate it if this commemoration is not accompanied by a reflection on our history at this key moment of 1492, and a healthy rejection of its myths and legends.

Translated by Peter Bush

Notes on Authors

Miguel Angel Asturias dominated writing in his native Guatemala in the 1930s and 1940s. His novels *El Señor Presidente* and *Hombres de maíz* (*Men of Maize*) are landmarks in the creation of a contemporary Latin American literature; Asturias was awarded the Nobel Prize for Literature in 1967. The story in this collection is taken from his *Leyendas de Guatemala*. Miguel Angel Asturias died in Madrid in 1974.

Alfredo Bryce Echenique was born in Lima in 1939. After studying at university in Peru, he went to live in Paris for many years. He is the author of several novels which are well-known in Latin America, including *Un mundo para Julius, Tantas veces Pedro, El hombre que hablaba de Octavia de Cádiz* and *La vida exagerada de Martín Romaña*, as well as many volumes of short stories. "Slice of Life" was originally published as "Una tajada de vida" in *Magdalena Peruana y otros cuentos*.

Julio Cortázar was an Argentine writer born in Brussels. He left Argentina in protest at the Peronist government in the early 1950s and lived for many years in Paris. In 1963 he wrote the novel *Rayuela* (*Hopscotch*), which became a classic of modern Latin American prose and inspired several generations of young Latin American writers. He also wrote many volumes of short stories, including *All Fires the Fire, Bestiary* and *We Love Glenda so Much*. Julio Cortázar died in France in 1984.

Ariel Dorfman was born in Chile in 1942, and was brought up there and in the United States. He became famous in Latin America in the early 1970s thanks to a book of popular sociology entitled *How to Read Donald Duck*, but has since become more widely known internationally for his novels — which include *Widows* and *Hard Rain* — and for his recent extremely successful play *Death and the Maiden*, which looks at the consequences of the violence of the Pinochet dictatorship years in Chile. "Warning" is taken from the volume of short stories *Cuentos casi completos*.

Carlos Fuentes is Mexico's best-known and most influential novelist. Born in 1928, he has produced a stream of novels and essays since the 1950s. His early novel *The Death of Artemio Cruz* remains one of his most powerful works, while *Christopher Unborn* and a recent television series *The Buried Mirror* represent his most immediate responses to the 500th anniversary celebrations.

Juan Goytisolo, the Spanish novelist, has always championed heterodox views of Spanish culture and ideas. Born in 1931, he left Franco's Spain in the mid 1950s, and has lived in Paris ever since. His works such as the trilogy of novels *Marks of Identity, Count Julian* and *Juan the Landless* (published by Serpent's Tail) explore the dissident, Arab tradition and the impact it has had on Spain. He recently completed a series of twenty programmes on Islam for Spanish television.

Daniel Moyano was born in Buenos Aires, Argentina, in 1930. His novels and short stories were often set in the Argentine interior, where Moyano lived for many years. After the military coup in 1976, he was imprisoned, and then left to live in exile in Spain, where he died in 1992. He wrote several novels, including *The Devil's Trill* (published by Serpent's Tail) and *The Flight of the Tiger*.

Juan José Saer is from Santa Fe, in the Rosario province of Argentina. He moved to Paris at 1968 at the age of thirty, and now teaches Argentine literature at the University of Rennes. Serpent's Tail has published one of his early novels, *The Witness*; Saer has written some twenty more.

Pedro Shimose is from Bolivia. Better known as a poet than a prose writer, his works are often set in the eastern lowlands of Bolivia, where he was born in 1940. He now lives in Madrid, and has recently published a volume of collected poetry.

Roberto Urías is a Cuban writer, born in Havana in 1959. He works as an editor for the magazine *Casa de las Américas*. His book of short stories *¿Porque llora Leslie Caron?* is to be published in Cuba soon.

Ana Valdés was born in Montevideo, Uruguay in 1953. She was arrested by the military authorities in 1972, and spent four years in jail for "subversive" activities. Since 1978 she has lived in Sweden. She has published several volumes of short stories, including *Después de Alicia* and *El Intruso*. 'The Peace of the Dead' is from her latest volume of short fiction *El Intruso*, which has appeared in Swedish but not as yet in Spanish.

Luisa Valenzuela is an Argentine novelist and short story writer. While she was living in the United States during the period of military dictatorship in Argentina at the end of the 1970s her work became known to an international audience. Her novel, *The Lizard's Tail*, and a book of short fiction, *Open Door*, are both published by Serpent's Tail.

Ana Lydia Vega is a Puerto Rican writer and professor of literature. "Pateco's Little Prank" is from the volume *Encancaranublado y otros cuentos de naufragio*, which won her the Cuban *Casa de las Américas* prize.